THE TWELFTH OF NEVER

THE TWELFTH OF NEVER

THE NEVER TRILOGY
BOOK ONE

OJÉ KENDI

Charlotte, NC

FALSTAFF
BOOKS

WWW.FALSTAFFBOOKS.COM

To my lovely wife,
Sheika.
My toughest critic
and my most devoted supporter.

Yesterday is history, tomorrow is a mystery, today is a gift...

— ELEANOR ROOSEVELT

Don't be so sure of that...

— NAOMI DOVE

PROLOGUE

Ezra Finkel was quite certain his life was about to end.

Ezra was also quite certain it would end badly.

He was going to die here, on this mountainside road, and now, on this cold winter evening, knowing his splattered blood would paint the crimson tale of his violent demise on the pristine white of the newly fallen snow.

That would be dreadful–about as dreadful as things could get, but what made it worse for Ezra was knowing that his blood would also paint its wretched tale throughout the somewhat less than pristine interior of his dusty old, yet well-loved car.

When Ezra was a much younger man and on assignment with an investigative journalist in East Asia, he had been unfortunate enough to witness a monk commit self-immolation as a demonstration against the government persecution of Buddhists. He found himself transfixed by shock and revulsion as he watched this horrid protest turned sacrifice play itself out. It ended with the burning man's skin dripping from his bones like fetid candle wax, and his ruined eyes bursting with an audible pop as they vacated their sockets before running down his cracked and charred cheeks. That had been a horrible death, but Ezra had been present during many horrible deaths before, having narrowly survived the Holocaust. As early as the tender age of fifteen, he had seen people in forced labor factories waste away from lack of nourishment until they were little more than a curtain of wrinkled skin loosely draped over the gnarled frames of their bulging skeletons. He had seen people poisoned by their own gangrenous limbs, because they could not give their numerous wounds the medical care they required and were unable to make an adequate separation between where they slept and where they defecated. He had seen people shot. He had seen people hanged. He had even seen people gutted and left to wallow in anguish as they made feeble attempts to keep the flies from hatching maggots in their exposed intestines, yet he still considered that burning monk's death to be the most unpleasant he had ever witnessed, until today.

As he struggled against the paralyzing weight of his own fear, Ezra amended his belief. He now decided that being dragged out of a vehicle kicking and screaming by a wolf whose unbelievable size surpassed that of a grizzly bear, and then torn apart and eaten by said wolf while still alive and aware enough to feel it, would surely be worse than burning, and unfortunately, this was the very death that lay before him now. Hoping against hope that he might change this ghastly fate, Ezra made a last attempt to back his car out of the snowbank he had skidded into moments ago.

It was a wasted effort.

Despite his overwhelming dread, or perhaps because of it, an amusing thought crossed Ezra's mind as he looked up from where he sat, into the piercing yellow eyes of the enormous creature looming just outside. He recalled when one of his closest friends commented on how much he suited his car. "Some people grow to resemble their dogs," his friend had remarked. "But you, Finkel… you've somehow grown to resemble that little Fiat 500 of yours." As absurd as it sounded, Ezra had to admit how oddly true that statement had been. Indeed, his attachment to the vehicle that his late wife purchased so very long ago, did suggest the kind of relationship one might have with a cherished pet, and Ezra often found himself thinking of it as an old companion rather than a mere means of transportation. Thus, no matter how small, outdated, or slow it was, he could not bring himself to replace it, and though he knew there was no point in regretting it now, he found himself wishing he had been driving something less like a chew toy for the nightmarish beast currently staring at him. *Perhaps one of those Panzers that Krupp forced us to build for der Führer,* Ezra thought, chuckling mirthlessly, because as far as keeping the thing out was concerned, anything less than a tank would provide as much protection as a cardboard box in a gunfight. He slumped back in his seat with a somber sigh of resignation and folded his hands in his lap as he waited patiently for his inevitable end, wondering if the last thing he would feel would be those inch-long teeth burying themselves in his throat, before tearing it out.

Like a drowning victim whose final thoughts are haunted by the earlier time when they were safe and dry, Ezra was astounded by how quickly life could take a turn for the worst. But his mistake hadn't been an unfortunate tumble from a fast-moving boat. His mistake had been the choice to swerve right instead of left to avoid the four-legged monstrosity standing in the middle of the road. Yes, swerving left would have put him in danger of a collision with an oncoming vehicle, or caused a loss of control that could have sent him careening over the cliff's edge, but those kinds of ends would have been preferable to being stuck in a snowbank while waiting to be devoured.

Ezra continued to stare at the wolf, feeling more and more like a frightened child with each passing second. Eventually, the monstrous thing leaned closer to the driver's side window, likely sizing up its next kill. For a moment, its enormous lupine face was partially obscured from view by the fog of its warm breath against the cold glass, yet the sounds of its heavy growling pant remained, being almost as resonant as the hum of the idling motor. As if realizing what it had done to remove its prey from immediate sight, the beast took a few steps back, allowing the vapor to fade. *Next comes the crouch*, Ezra thought, *then the pounce, then no more me.* He closed his eyes and whispered the Shema prayer in preparation for the end of his life, but he was interrupted by something other than the sound of shattering glass he had expected. He was shocked out of his muttering, and nearly out of his life, when he heard the creature speak.

"Come out, Ezra."

Though he had never considered himself to be a particularly brave fellow, he knew he was far from a coward, yet hearing those three words brought out a fear unlike any the old man had ever experienced before. Yes, he had suffered greatly during the war, as did countless others, but he hadn't allowed it to break him. He had lived his life humbly and unhurriedly, comforted by the knowledge that his mind had been dependably well-anchored in reality, until now. His disbelief in the supernatural had suspended enough to accept that a wolf could grow to such massive proportions, but to accept that the thing had just spoken? Surely not. Such lips had no business parting to form words, he told himself, so perhaps it was time to admit that he might finally be losing his mind.

Still, as unnerved as he was, he managed to detect something somewhat familiar about the enormous wolf's voice, and in an ironic twist of fate, it was that hint of familiarity that helped keep Ezra from falling apart entirely. Vaguely aware of the disconcerting implications involved, Ezra swore he heard his own mother's voice woven into what sounded like an echoing chorus of lost children coming from the creature's throat. Along with being an unexpected source of stability against the very fear it was inspiring, the beast's words also served to bring about a revelation in Ezra's mind. This revelation was immediately followed by immense relief.

"But of course," he said in his usual languid tone. "You are a dream, are you not? Or more correctly, you are a nightmare. How else could you know my name or mimic the voice of my dearest *Eema*; may her memory ever be a blessing? How else could you be so unnaturally large? How else could you even speak, for that matter?"

Though somewhat familiar with what he had heard referred to as lucid dreams, Ezra was certain he had never experienced one before. Most of his dreams fled his mind the moment he raised his head from the pillow. The rare few he could remember tended to be like old television sitcoms: short, simple, and lacking in color, allowing no input from the observer. Hence, he found the level of detail in this current dream quite off-putting. Never, in either dream or nightmare, could he remember feeling the itchy wool of his sweater scratching the tender skin on the back of his neck, but he could now. Never could he recall smelling anything at all in a dream, yet he could sense the thickly sweet aroma of coffee hanging in the confined air of the tiny Fiat. He was amazed to find that he could even remember inconsequential events, such as his brief stop at the eye doctor earlier today.

"Or..." he mused, "perhaps I did not just stop there briefly. Perhaps I am still at the eye doctor this very moment, asleep in the waiting room with that tattered copy of the Reader's Digest on my knee."

Now that he had spoken of this possibility aloud, he knew it had to be the truth of the matter. It wouldn't explain the incredibly realistic feelings and smells, but it would explain the giant talking she-wolf. Ezra was jarred from these thoughts when once again the beast spoke.

"Come out, Ezra. Now."

Yes, Ezra reluctantly admitted. That was definitely his mother's voice he heard accompanying, or perhaps even leading, the many others emanating from the creature's throat. There was no mistaking her woeful yet commanding tone, and Ezra thought it was quite fitting that his subconscious would substitute the aspect of a giant she-wolf as the representation of the brash and occasionally overbearing matriarch from his early childhood. It was that presence alone that assured Ezra he was safe. This was because he knew without a doubt that no matter what form she took, his mother, who had willingly given her life to protect her family, would never harm her only son. This all probably amounted to nothing more than a bad gefilte fish induced fantasy anyway, he told himself, and didn't people wake up long before anything truly awful happened in nightmares? Of course they did, he thought, and with that in mind, feigning a level of confidence he in no way felt, Ezra opened the door and stepped out.

The frosty chill of the season hit him immediately, and Ezra instinctively pulled his goose down parka closed against it, while adding *feeling cold* to the growing list of things that had never happened to him before in a dream. Now that he stood face to face with the she-wolf, its height making that point quite literal, Ezra was amazed to find that he could see a bit of genuine beauty in the disturbing creature. Its imposing size, its silver-white fur, and its moon-yellow eyes gave it a quality unquestionably terrible, yet also awe-inspiring, like the frothy rapids of a storm-swollen river, or an oncoming avalanche. The she-wolf stared unblinkingly at Ezra for several uncomfortably long seconds, before giving the slightest of nods and then turning to walk back toward the middle of the road. After a brief hesitation, Ezra followed, sensing it was what the beast wanted. As he walked, he wondered whether she had been judging him during those silent seconds of staring, and he felt a peculiar sense of contentment from the knowledge that he had been allowed to dwell in this dream a little longer. A few steps brought the unlikely pair to the place in the road where Ezra had been forced to swerve to avoid hitting the she-wolf, and what he saw there shocked all remaining fear out of him.

Sprawled on the ground like a heap of discarded laundry lay the body of a girl who looked slightly younger than the age Ezra had been when the Nazis kidnapped his family. She was petite, honey brown-skinned, and dressed in what appeared to be the local private school uniform, though not much else. She was also missing one of her shoes. Her tiny face was partially obscured by a cascading bush of dark curly hair. Through it, Ezra could see the unmistakable shock in her wide staring eyes. Whatever it was that happened to her, she clearly hadn't expected it.

Even in his bewildered state, Ezra noted that the child's attire was utterly inadequate for a snowy winter day such as this. Yet she did not appear to be suffering any ill effects, at least not as far as the temperature was concerned. A thin blanket of snow covered the surrounding road, yet almost none on the child herself. This suggested the she-wolf had been standing over her, or perhaps it had curled itself around her, as protection against any oncoming cars as well as the winter chill. Ezra was dismayed to see that the exposed skin on the girl's face, arms, and legs was riddled with a myriad of small cuts and bruises. This, coupled with the twinkling black shards of tinted glass strewn across the road hinted how she came to be here, yet there were no other cars in the area excluding his own. In fact, as far as Ezra could tell, the only evidence that any type of vehicle had passed this way recently, other than the broken glass, was a couple of deeply set yet quickly fading tire tracks in the snowbank just a few feet ahead of his Fiat. Had it been a hit and run then, he wondered?

With some difficulty, due to the weight of his heavy coat and the ache in his old bones, Ezra lowered himself to kneel beside the child. He reached out and touched her cheek, and he was both surprised and relieved to find her warm. After adjusting his glasses to get a better look at her, he also noted that her tiny chest was moving up and down, but only slightly. The girl clung to life by a thread.

"Surely she came from a car," Ezra remarked, turning to speak to the she-wolf as if it were just another bystander. "After all, she would not have been walking on this mountain road alone in the cold, with one bare foot and no coat, would she?"

With a silent gesture, the she-wolf brought the old man's attention to a distant section of the guardrail that had been violently torn away. Something quite a bit larger than either the Fiat or the beast must have plowed through the wood and steel and careened down the steep mountain slope beyond. Nearby, a pink tasseled scarf hung from a jutting scrap of metal, swaying in the breeze like a windsock, marking the dreadful site with a bit of color against the stark white of the snow. Fearing that there might be other victims, Ezra stood and started to make his way to the broken guardrail, yet he immediately halted when the she-wolf stepped forward to bar his path.

"Get the child to safety," the creature commanded. *"The others are gone."*

"But how do I do that?" Ezra asked, completely forgetting that this was all just a dream. "My car... it is stuck in the snowbank."

Without commenting, the she-wolf turned and walked over to the Fiat, which Ezra thought looked even smaller in comparison to the beast, now that he was seeing both from the outside. The she-wolf took the rear bumper in its jaws and pulled the car out of the snowdrift with absurd ease. It then returned to Ezra, who was mulling over the interesting tale he would have to tell if anyone ever asked how a row of dents resembling giant tooth marks found their way onto the metal bumper of his car. As before, the beast interrupted his thoughts with its words, this time by repeating its earlier command.

"Get the child to safety."

"I will," Ezra vowed. "We will go straight to Weldon Memorial. It is close by, and I have friends who are doctors there." After taking a brief glance down at the child, he added, "Though I am not the man I once was. Perhaps you could help me get her into the car?"

The care and delicacy the beast used to lift the child in its jaws filled Ezra with an unexpected emotional warmth, and he chided himself for his thoughtlessness as he scrambled to open the passenger door and lower the backrest of the seat. There was a moment where the Fiat shook with the beast's efforts, and from where Ezra stood, it looked like it was trying to squeeze itself into the vehicle. When the moment passed, the she-wolf stepped away to reveal the child lying perfectly situated in the reclined passenger seat. To the old man's amazement, it had even somehow managed to buckle the seat-belt. It then turned its oddly wizened gaze to the car's owner.

"Many thanks," Ezra said.

The she-wolf gave the slightest of nods in response and then turned to leave. In spite of his earlier fear, Ezra was reluctant to see it go. Finally coming to the realization that his mind was incapable of this level of imagination, he asked, "This is not a dream after all, or even a nightmare, is it?"

The she-wolf turned back to him, and in its eyes, Ezra witnessed the deepest sorrow he had ever seen in his life. *"All of reality is a nightmare,"* the creature replied. *"Our choices have polluted this existence with unending horrors, and we have driven the dreamer to madness. This is why we suffer."*

And with that, the beast loped off into the nearby wood, vanishing amongst the trees, leaving neither tracks nor trace that it had ever been.

1

Graham was disturbed.

Now that he had correctly identified the feeling, there was no point in denying it. He had always done his level best to avoid what his mother had referred to as navel gazing, feeling it was a general waste of time, but today he couldn't stop himself. Some irresistible urge demanded a bit of soul searching on this cold winter morning, and he reluctantly gave in.

His fifty-plus years as an officer of the law had supplied Graham with a distasteful cornucopia of unwelcomed emotions. Of these, fear was the most common and considering how often his job required that he place himself in danger, he supposed it was understandable. It was unacceptable in his humble opinion, and it was undesirable, but it was also understandable. Now, as he sat peering through the windshield at the morning sun glinting off the newly fallen snow stubbornly clinging to the hood of his patrol car, he recognized a relatively new emotion invading his usual air of cynical indifference.

Now, he was disturbed.

"Something's wrong in my town," Graham muttered to himself, turning to stare out of the driver's side window at what he could see of the small municipality as he drove on.

He crept by small tucked away neighborhoods populated by stately Colonials, and lonely streets with a smattering of standalone Carriage houses, with occasional tendrils of smoke drifting lazily from their chimneys. He even passed a sprawling gable-roofed Victorian, which, while not necessarily the oldest home in the area, was the only one openly displaying its cotton plantation history. Using this route to reach the county seat always put him in a Mayberry frame of mind as far as television analogies go, but if asked, he would have said that today his feelings were a little closer to *The Twilight Zone*. It was cold but seasonably so, with a sky that held a somber ashen cloud cover so thick, it made morning feel more like dusk. The streets and sidewalks were ominously clear of traffic, both vehicular and pedestrian, and the recent sprinkling of snow made everything appear uncharacteristically clean. This false neatness was usually enough to raise Graham's spirits, if only slightly, but not this morning, because this morning something was wrong in his town.

One of the things which hinted at the wrongness was the many pumpkins Graham noted decorating the windows and the stoops of various homes and businesses he passed. *No, not pumpkins,* he corrected. *You'd have to refer to those as jack-o'-lanterns, because regular old pumpkins don't have impish grins carved into them. But why am I even seeing them,* he wondered? *Why the hell haven't people thrown those damn things out like they were supposed to a month ago?* Was this some new small-town joke which had escaped his notice until now, or had some people just decided that they should forgo Christmas this year, and instead try a second helping of Halloween? *And just how the hell had the things not rotted away to nothing by now anyway*, he wondered? People definitely weren't growing any new pumpkins in this weather, so these had to be months old.

Still, as curious as he was about these oddities, they weren't enough to make him want to stop and interrogate the owner of the next home or business he came across displaying a grinning gourd, because these were just a symptom of the wrongness. They weren't the cause. They were merely a side piece.

"A side piece?" he had once been asked in a tone of jovial surprise by someone much younger, who had attached their own generation's far more lewd definition to the phrase. "A side piece to the puzzle, moron," he had responded, before taking a moment to explain. "When I'm collecting clues to a case, or to any given mystery, it helps to categorize them as either side pieces or middle pieces, in a hypothetical puzzle whose parts have been mixed with any number of other puzzles, and whose box I've misplaced. Side pieces with their obvious edges are like minor clues: easy to locate, easy to connect, and effective when boundaries needed to be established, but not much help in discovering what the overall picture was meant to be. Middle pieces are like vital clues, which are essential to giving you the real picture, or solving the case. The middle ones are also far more difficult to discover and connect, but once I'm able to create a decent frame using side pieces, it becomes much easier to recognize and properly place the middle ones."

Thus, he wouldn't be stopping to question anyone about the jack-o'-lanterns, because it would likely only lead him to another side piece, if it led to anything at all. Besides, he was exhausted, having worked through the entire night. Barring any unforeseen emergencies, the only home he would be stopping at would be his own, just after leaving the only business he would be stopping at, which also happened to be his own, or at least the one he had been elected to for yet another term. After all these years as sheriff, he still found it baffling that the people of his town continued to believe that a lonely seventy-three-year-old bachelor could keep the local ne'er-do-wells in order. With little else to do other than grumble about the inaccuracies he noted while watching *Law & Order*, feed and water his lazy mutt dog, and catch the occasional troublemaker, he vowed to continue the job to the best of his ability until the bitter end.

Unfortunately, despite what the voters might think, that end would probably come in about two years, to the undoubted delight of Mayor Beckett, when, if Georgia state customs were to be abided by, Graham would be nudged into retirement through being bestowed the Honorary Sheriff Emeritus award. It was an empty title, however historically significant, meant to get stubborn old farts like him out of the way of younger and supposedly more exciting new candidates who just couldn't seem to win elections, like the mayor's nephew. This would ensure that Graham would be forced to limit aiming his grumpy rants at his pooch, his television, or the eternally sluggish pizza delivery people.

Just once though, before he made that final curtain call, he wanted to do something that truly mattered. He wanted to stop something horrible from happening before it happened, not come in afterward to pick up the pieces of a victim's broken life while attempting to administer some sad semblance of justice, as most law enforcement officers seemed destined to do. Still, entering the story after the fact was occasionally worth it if he could put an end to another person's suffering. Yet if last night was any indication of how his professional life would come to a close, he would be cleaning up the remains of poor unfortunate motorists from country mountainside roads, and then spend many fruitless hours attempting to hunt down their nefarious hit-and-run drivers.

"Careful what you wish for, hoss," he muttered to himself. "Because you're never too old to get shot in the–"

A sudden loud and hollow sounding thump on his passenger side door caused Graham to stomp his brake pedal. The car would have come to a screeching halt if he had been going any faster. As it was, the creeping progress he had been making meant that the stop made hardly any noise at all, other than the mild squeak of the brakes, announcing they would soon need a mechanic's attention.

"God damn kids…" Graham growled as he put the car in park then opened the door. The winter wind immediately invaded the vehicle, swirling uncomfortably around his neck and ears as if it had been angered by his attempts to keep it out, making him thankful for the county-issued fleece parka he was wearing.

He grunted while shifting his weight to one side to make standing and exiting the car easier. This also required him to rock back once and then forward before he could free himself from the seat, which added just enough time to the process to make spotting the prankster who decided it would be fun to throw a snowball or an egg at the "Pigs" doubtful.

Or 5-O or whatever the hell it is that they're calling us these days, he thought, scowling.

He glanced over the hood of the car in the direction the projectile had come, hoping that the stark white of his surroundings would make locating any bit of fleeing color easier. There was no movement at all in the direction he was certain that the offending object had come. There weren't even any tell-tale signs of disturbed snow betraying where the brat had been hiding or where they were headed. The only things moving were the occasional snowflake falling from the sky, the nearby branches of a leafless tree swaying in the breeze, and the lingering mist from his own breath hanging in the frosty air.

He also heard nothing except for the gentle murmur of his idling motor. The lack of sounds was more vexing than the lack of sights, because if history had taught him anything, all such incidents were accompanied by retreating laughter if the perpetrator was alone or retreating laughter and offensive jeers if they had accomplices. Yet there was nothing.

Grumbling about this generation having far too many delinquents in need of a swift kick in the rear end, he turned to lower himself back into the cab of the vehicle after deciding he would wait to assess the damage to or defacement of his door when he got back to the station. An odd little noise he could not quite identify came from the other side of his car, causing him to freeze in the process of bending over. If he were asked to guess, he would have said the sound he heard resembled a small child with a bit of a cold, whispering something unintelligible. *But I didn't hit a kid*, he assured himself. *Not going twenty miles an hour, I didn't. Not even in this weather.* Besides, there had been no one anywhere in sight the entire morning. Every street he passed had been eerily vacant, including this one. Feeling the slightest hint of trepidation despite his certainty, he straightened up with a grunt of displeasure and notable difficulty and then trudged through the half-melted ice-slush in the road around the front of the vehicle to the passenger side.

Lying there in the snow on the ground near the door, twitching uncontrollably from the apparent pain of its injuries, was a large black bird. Though black wasn't quite the right description for the winged creature, Graham thought. This crow, or raven, or whatever it was, looked blacker than black to him. What he was seeing may have been a trick of the light, or it may have been due to the extreme contrast of the bird's ebon feathers against the stark white of the snow, but to Graham it was more like a quivering bird-shaped absence of space. A feathery negative. A spot where God had plucked a thread from the quilt of existence, leaving an avian-esque hole through which the endless nothingness of the starless void could be seen.

Graham blinked, wondering where such strangely poetic thoughts had come, because they surely hadn't come from him. He had to have read that somewhere, though considering he didn't read much more than the newspaper, he doubted it, unless the local rag had taken a more fanciful slant recently. He briefly closed his eyes and gave his head a brisk shake to clear his mind of the fug of the long night clouding it and then took another look. He was relieved to find that his next glance down was considerably less disturbing.

The creature was just an unremarkable black bird after all, albeit a large one, whose head, he now noted, was cocked at an unnatural angle. With reality having reasserted itself, if indeed it had been absent at all, a new and more familiar emotion arose within the old man.

"Well, just what the hell were you thinking?" he growled at the dying bird, while gesturing to a spot on the car where a small dent dusted by a bit of ebon fluff could clearly be seen. "There's no way on earth you didn't see me. I was barely moving for Christ's sake! And why the hell aren't you someplace warmer?"

As if it was attempting to offer an answer, the bird gave another somewhat weaker squawk than it had a moment ago, but with Graham being closer, the sound was much clearer.

"three… six… five… three… twelfth."

Graham stared down at the bird, open mouthed and

astonished. It wasn't that it had spoken which rattled him, because he knew many birds could be taught to speak. He even vaguely recalled being told that ravens and crows were some of the most intelligent birds out there, as well as being some of the best talkers, though they rarely had the desire or the opportunity to display such skills in front of people.

What bothered Graham was the troubling memory the bird's words evoked. That memory involved his mother's twin sister, the childless and reclusive Aunt Agatha, who according to his mother had as well as wiped her ass with the Good Lord's mandates and the family's decent standing in the community, by becoming the mistress of the wealthy man whose children she had been nannying. The discovery of her illicit relationship ended Agatha's career as an adulterous au-pair, while also bringing to light how she had been able to afford the curiously opulent aviary she had constructed inside her home, which she had stocked with many exotic-hued budgerigars (she had absolutely refused to call them parakeets). A few months after Aunt Agatha's dirty secret became common knowledge, she unexpectedly fell victim to an errant illness (likely flu-induced pneumonia), forcing a much younger Graham and his mother Agnes to make several trips to Aunt Agatha's home to get her final affairs in order.

It was during one such trip that they received an unexpected visit from the female half of the marriage Agatha nearly ended. The wealthy man's wife had come demanding to know where the home-wrecking hussy she once trusted with her children had hidden all the money that her idiot husband had given her. This woman, who had not been told that Agatha had a twin or that she had recently passed away, directed all her demands and all her fury toward the woman she believed to be responsible for her anguish. Graham's mother, well known for her short temper, had no idea what the silly twit was talking about, nor did she care (at least not then), all which she made explicitly clear as she chased the woman off the property at the point of her sister's old shotgun. Agnes did, however, know that her sister had never trusted banks, and had a habit of secreting her few valuables all over her house.

That unexpected intrusion from her sister's former employer gave significance to another bit of knowledge which his mother had previously believed to be meaningless. An uncharacteristic grin slowly spread across Agnes's face when she combined the new possibility of a cache being hidden somewhere in the home, with the knowledge that a few of her sister's birds could speak.

"Can't get the damn things to shut the hell up," Agnes had grumbled to herself. *"Polly want a fucking cracker*, and *Who's a shitty bird*, and on and on..." But Agnes could recall three birds standing out from the flock. Calling her son from the nearby room where he had been boxing up some of Agnes's old things, she demanded that he remind her what the birds had been squawking that first day they arrived.

"Umm..." Graham remembered saying, giving the matter some thought. "Whose a pretty–"

"No, idiot boy!" she had shouted impatiently, causing him to flinch. "I mean the ones that was saying the numbers! Remember?"

"Sorry momma," he said, which was a phrase he could recall repeating constantly in his younger days. "That first one said something like, 'three,' then 'uh oh,' then 'kitchen.'"

"Yes!" Agnes had said, sounding almost feverish with anticipation. "Like it was mimicking what it heard Aggy say on a day she was counting her cooking mistakes." With a jab of a finger in her son's direction, she added, "But then there was the one that said, 'seven, uh oh,' and something, and another that said 'nine, uh oh,' and something else, only we assumed they was speaking gibberish because of the first one!"

That said, Agnes hitched up her dress and trotted off in the direction of the kitchen with an avaricious glint in her eye, shoving her son aside as she passed. Having no desire to follow, Graham returned to the work he had been doing in the dining room. After what felt like hours of hearing his mother sling pots and pans haphazardly around the kitchen, as well as slinging a few choice profane phrases, Graham was startled out of his work by his mother's slightly maniacal sounding laughter.

Hurrying into the room, Agnes shoved a dusty old envelope under Graham's nose, saying, "Take yourself a gander!"

He did so and was shocked to find that the envelope was full of twenty-dollar bills.

"Three hundred dollars," his mother said, sparing him the necessity of counting. Noting the blank look on her son's face, she added, "It wasn't saying 'uh oh.' It was saying Oh, oh! Three, oh, oh, in the kitchen, you pudding head."

But Agnes had misread young Graham's expression, and it wasn't until she followed his gaze to the nearby trash bag that she understood. This was the point where Agnes's uncharacteristic grin began to falter, before eventually fading back into her customary scowl.

"Shit," she muttered. "Which one was that?"

"I think it was the one that said, 'nine, oh, oh, something,'" Graham answered.

"Course it was," Agnes sighed, openly disgusted.

Graham didn't need to be a mind reader to know what his mother was thinking, because he had been thinking the same thing. That first day they arrived, they had been focused on collecting anything of value in the home, which might be used to offset the cost of Agatha's funeral. Minutes into the search Agnes had become quite annoyed by the constant chatter of the birds, which she had always hated, and after telling Graham to open the front door, she took perverse delight in snatching each one from their enormous cage and throwing them bodily out the home.

Noting the shocked look on her son's face, yet not hesitating in her task, she shouted, "Who the hell is gonna feed and care for them then, huh? You?"

She scoffed when he remarked that he could do exactly that, and her rising temper coupled with her atrocious aim left the next bird she threw horribly crippled, when, instead of sailing through the open archway, it smacked headlong into the doorframe with a sickening crunch. Not known for having an abundance of compassion, Agnes had at least summoned enough empathy to snap the poor broken thing's neck.

Prior to this incident, the birds had been allowing Agnes to collect them with little effort on her part, likely due to her resemblance to their deceased owner. Once they were aware of their new and potentially deadly fate, however, they began to put up more of a fight, flitting around their cage and dodging her clumsy groping hands. Eventually, all of Aunt Agatha's pets had been "returned to the wilds what spawned 'em," as Agnes so eloquently put it, and the corpse of the one who had met his end at the edge of the door jamb was tossed unceremoniously into the nearest garbage bag.

Those tiny feathery recipients of Graham's mother's ire had not appreciated being evicted from their home, but they would have the last laugh, because if Agnes was correct, and her discovery in the kitchen seemed to bear this out, then one of the ones she had "returned to the wilds" had been taught the hidden location of seven hundred dollars, and the one whose brains she had dashed out, had been taught the hidden location of another nine hundred. And neither Agnes nor her son could recall what the two locations were which they had heard the birds utter.

"Sixteen hundred dollars!" Agnes screamed at the walls after several fruitless days of tearing the house apart in her search for the money. "We shared a God-damned womb for nine months, Aggy, and you couldn't put aside your bullshit long enough to tell me that highfalutin son of a bitch gave you a pile of money!"

That declaration had almost forced a laugh out of young Graham, which would have been a grievous mistake given his mother's sour mood. Having spent many a clandestine hour in his aunt's company, whose kindness he truly cherished, Graham knew that it was his mother's "bullshit" that had created the wall which separated the two sisters, not his aunt's. That wall's numerous bricks were conjured from the two sisters' endless arguments over what Agatha called her sister's revolting opinion of anyone that didn't look like she did.

"I'll never understand how you escaped being poisoned by my sister's idiocy, Joey," he recalled her once saying to him in his late teen years. No one else called him Joey but her, and he liked it that way. "I'm ever so glad you did, though," she continued, "but I knew her and that brainless father of yours would never allow you to court that pretty colored girl you were sweet on. Not with their connections to the Klan and all." He could also remember her giving him a somewhat lecherous wink, before adding, "A real shame too. You would have had such beautiful babies. All the little octoroon ones always are. If I believed in God, I'd say that was his way of telling us we should set aside our differences and get together."

Graham never had the heart to correct his aunt by telling her that any children he might have had with that "colored girl" would have been one half black, not one eighth, or that terms such as colored, and octoroon were considered offensive by the people they were meant to define. Regardless, she had been correct about his parents. They hadn't allowed it, and eventually, the wedge which had separated sister from sister, grew to separate mother from son…

Graham shook his head to clear his mind and drag himself out of the past. "Well, you brought out an epic bit of navel gazing, didn't you?" he said to the twitching black bird lying in the snowy slush. "Haven't thought about Aunt Agatha in a coon's age." A scowl, not unlike that of his mother's, creased his brow as he contemplated his next actions. "Now what am I to do with–"

Graham stopped midsentence as a nearby sound caught his attention. He whirled around, much slower and far less gracefully than he would have liked, while instinctively putting his hand on the butt of his revolver. What he saw caused him to take a step back in surprise, and he came within inches of trampling the injured bird as he struggled to remove his gun from its holster. Later, he would thank God that the faulty button on his retention strap kept him from pulling out the weapon. As frayed as his nerves were at that moment, he probably would have shot what he saw standing on the nearby snow-covered sidewalk, and no amount of love from the voters could have removed his ass from that sling. Still, anyone seeing what he saw might have also reached for the nearest weapon with the fullest of intentions to use it.

What Graham saw was a small person apparently masquerading as a mentally unstable clown, holding a leash attached to a small horse apparently masquerading as a mentally unstable dog.

At least, that was what his sleep-deprived mind was telling him as it struggled to make sense of things.

The dog, whose pinkish paleness made Graham sure it

had to be an albino, and whose girth made him think it must have been one of those short-haired mastiff breeds, outweighed its owner by at least sixty pounds or more. That dog wasn't the one being walked. The child was. The openly threatening look in the canine's storm-cloud tinted eyes made it abundantly clear that if it wished, it could bring a violent end to Graham's life, owner be damned. Its frightening visage was made freakish by the numerous scars overlapping its body, giving it a *stitched together by Dr. Frankenstein* appearance. As if to complete the mad pet guise, around its neck was a thick black collar where Graham could just make out the words: Lest Ye Be Vexed. Surely that isn't its name, Graham thought, though considering what he was seeing, he wouldn't have been surprised to find that it was.

Still, as unsettling a view as it was, the intimidating beast took the second-place prize for the most unsettling of the pair. The main reason for this conclusion was that Graham was no fan of clowns. He didn't suffer from coulrophobia, he just didn't care for people who wore anything obscuring their face, particularly while they roamed around a quiet residential neighborhood with no circus in sight.

But this pint-sized jester, whose obsidian-black and bone white-garb likely put it in the twisted mime or demented Pierrot variety of clown, took its facial obscurement to a darker level. Why, Graham asked himself, did this child's mask look like a porcelain doll which someone had shattered with a hammer, and then haphazardly glued back together using blood? Why, he also asked himself, was its mouth set in an open "O" of surprise, as if it had seen that hammer coming, yet had been unable to avoid it? Why did it possess a single, disturbingly beautiful ice-blue eye, set beside a gaping void of an empty socket? And why, oh why, did some brainless idiot failure of a parent allow their child to leave the house wearing such a costume?

Graham forced himself to take several calming breaths to get himself under control. With deliberate care, he removed his hand from his gun and held it up to show it was empty, and that he meant no harm. Neither the child nor the dog reacted to this, other than the dog yawning as if it was bored. With the immediate danger of the moment having passed, he felt his earlier anger returning, yet he did his best to keep it contained because the potential danger, being that of the dog, remained.

"Halloween's long gone, youngster," Graham said, putting as much authority into his voice as he dared. "And it's a bad idea to walk around the neighborhood wearing a mask for no reason."

Both the child and the dog remained ominously silent, though the dog offered a slow blink.

"That...outfit...can't be near warm enough for weather like this," Graham said. With a nod to his patrol car, he added, "How 'bout you and your dog hop in back and I'll drive you home?" He wasn't thrilled about the prospect of having either of these two oddities sitting behind him while he drove, but he was curious about where they lived and who was responsible for them. While he thought the protective steel mesh gate separating the front of the car from the back would be enough to prevent any true shenanigans, he knew it would do nothing to keep it from being a thoroughly unpleasant journey.

Neither the child nor the dog responded to his offer, not that he expected any response from the dog, so Graham decided to coax them by opening the door. He was reaching for the door handle when a nearby croak reminded him why he had stopped in the first place.

"Twe..." the black bird whispered. "Twelfth..."

"Jesus," Graham groaned. "I forgot all about–"

The sound of tiny footsteps crunching in the snow

brought Graham's attention back to the child and the dog. The pair had recommenced their walk and were now several paces away. Graham considered calling after them, then thought better of it. He had already been on his way back to the precinct to deal with a supposed emergency before the bird had delayed him. His deputy wasn't the type to exaggerate, so he needed to get back to the office and deal with whatever it was that Emmett radioed him about. The kid seemed comfortable enough in the cold anyway, so he would worry about speaking to their negligent parents some other time.

"First things first though," he said, pulling a handkerchief from his pocket and glancing down at the bird. "It would be wrong to just leave you here like this." With an audible sigh, he slowly bent over, noting every ache and pain, and set to the regrettable yet necessary task of euthanasia. As Aunt Agatha had once told him while resigning herself to the same task with one of her own terminally ill birds, "God or no God, I'm certain all life is sacred, Joey. I'm also certain that letting something suffer needlessly, is profane."

It wasn't long before he was back in his patrol car headed to work. As he drove, he considered the last few minutes of his morning, which, interestingly enough, involved a talking bird whose earthly remains were now residing respectfully in his trunk, and a kid walking their monster dog while wearing a Halloween costume which was completely inappropriate for the current weather, much less the time of year. Two more side pieces in his mystery puzzle? He wasn't certain, which was frustrating, but there was one thing he was quite certain of. "Ain't even 9 a.m.," he muttered to himself. "And it's already turning out to be a pretty shitty day."

Hours later, while he was trying to avoid being gutted by

a knife wielding psycho, he would think back to saying this and realize it had been the understatement of the year.

Graham sighed heavily, as much from fatigue as from antipathy, while putting his car in park, having finally reached his destination. He glanced at the familiar building and wondered for what was surely the thousandth time, why the town decided that plastering faded red bricks around the exterior was a better idea than just tearing the obsolete structure down and starting from scratch. Muttering something about cheapskate penny-pinching mayors, he turned the car off, removed the keys, opened the door, and then began the ritual of rocking and shifting to make exiting easier. He knew he could stand to lose a few pounds, a fact common with most of the people of which he was acquainted, but he didn't consider himself to be fat. Not really. It was his knees that were the problem. They just weren't what they used to be, but whose knees were after over seventy years of near constant use?

"At least I have my health," he grunted with a smirk, making a mental note to rap his knuckles on the first piece of wood he saw. He shut the car door, hitched up his belt, and made his way into the building. Just inside the door, he was greeted by his chief deputy, Emmett.

Graham and Emmett differed in nearly every way, apart from gender. Emmett was a tall, slender, young black man with a pleasant smile that seemed to say, *I'm pretty sure everything is going to be okay.* Graham was a short, stout, older white man with a constant scowl that seemed to say, *everything had damn well better be okay.*

"There any coffee?" Graham muttered.

Emmett, who had obviously been expecting his boss, had

a hot cup waiting. He handed it to Graham, who accepted it, sipped it, and grunted appreciatively.

"Much obliged," Graham sighed. "Now what's this 'life-or-death emergency that I had best come see for myself'?"

Without comment, Emmett headed down the nearby hall after motioning for Graham to follow. Their destination was at the end of the hall, and once there Emmett nodded to a single paneled door. Graham peered through the one-way glass into the sparsely lit side-office that served as the precinct's sole interrogation room.

The scant furnishings within consisted of two rigidly uncomfortable metal chairs set at the head and foot of a rectangular table, which was small enough to allow two people seated at either end to reach across and hold hands if they wished. Settled in the chair facing the window, crouching intently over two small stacks of white paper, sat a girl of no more than twelve. Her tiny face, slightly obscured by a cascading bush of dark curly hair, was undoubtedly pretty under normal circumstances, but less so now because it was twisted into a mask of worry and concentration. The child's skin tone, Graham noted, eerily matched the cream-laden hue of his coffee. He also noticed that her attire, which seemed just a little too crisp and a little too clean, whispered a tale of wealth. It took him a moment, but once Graham placed the burgundy sweater vest, striped bow tie, and navy-blue pleated skirt of Heaton Academy (all barely seen beneath the child's red fur-trimmed parka and pink tasseled scarf) he knew his assessment had been correct. *If there ever existed an institution dedicated to educating the spawn of the rich and obnoxious*, Graham thought, *Heaton is definitely it.*

A quick flick of the girl's wrist as she flipped a sheet of paper from one stack to the next brought his attention to what she was doing. The girl briefly paused in her writing for what appeared to be a moment of contemplation before jotting a few words on the blank sheet of paper lying just beneath her chin with a large black marker. She then took a couple of seconds to scan her work before flipping it over to join the growing stack near her right elbow. Though her writing was large and clear, the sheets in the *elbow stack* were faced down, making them impossible to read from where the two men stood. One by one, the sheets departed from what Graham's mind had unconsciously labeled as the *chin stack*, to join their used fellows nearby. The girl was as swift as she was diligent, and the *elbow stack* grew considerably before Graham realized he had been completely captivated by watching her work.

It's because she's so focused, Graham thought. *She's writing as if her life depended on it.* Graham took a sip of his coffee, cleared his throat, and then spoke.

"Emmett, is the life-or-death emergency you called me back here to 'see for myself' located behind that little girl?"

"Well, no sir," Emmett replied apologetically. "The emergency *is* the little girl."

"Emmitt," Graham sighed, turning to scowl at his deputy. "I've been working all night."

"Yes, I kn–" Emmett began, but Graham interrupted.

"A night that included clearing a three-car pile-up."

"I know, but–"

"A three-car pile-up with fatalities."

"She knows things, Graham!" Emmett nearly shouted, giving a glance toward the window which made it clear he wished to avoid being overheard by their young guest. In a more reserved tone, he added, "Things she has no business knowing."

"Does she," Graham said, looking both annoyed and unconvinced. "Like what?"

"Like your social security number, for one, and mine." Emmett paused, perhaps hoping the silence would lend gravity to his words, or maybe he was just hoping for some kind of reaction. Graham only offered a blank stare, so Emmett went on. "She knows your address too… and mine."

"Well that fits, now don't it," Graham said, obviously unimpressed. "She'd have to know where we lived if she's been digging around in our trash for personal information." Watching Emmett shake his head emphatically, he added, "Or maybe she just hacked our computers. I hear that kind of thing is second nature to kids these days."

"She don't talk like a kid," Emmett said, now showing that something about the girl had him genuinely unnerved. "She can't be more than twelve or so, but I swear she sounds like she's thirty."

Graham waved the comment away. "That describes half the kids I know. They're all growing up too fast nowadays."

"She knows that my parents are distant cousins," Emmett said, glancing around as if the two men weren't alone in the hallway.

"I know that too," Graham said with an uncharacteristic chuckle.

"But no one else does," Emmett pointed out in a hoarse whisper.

"Pretty sure your parents know," Graham remarked, sipping his coffee. "And probably their parents as well. Maybe she found out from one of them."

"She knows that we looked the other way in the Dalton case," Emmett said flatly.

That statement awarded Emmett an enquiring glare from his boss. This time when Graham spoke, his words were slow and precise, and laced with an unquestionable edge of displeasure. "You been discussing the Dalton case, Emmett?"

"Course not!" Emmett said with a trace of wounded indignation. "You know I'd never."

"Because it'd mean our badges at the very least, if something like that got out," Graham said, still glowering. "Maybe even jail time."

"I know," Emmett insisted.

"I thought we were on the same page about that?"

"We are, Graham!"

"Then how exactly could that little girl, who incidentally had to be in diapers when Jasper Dalton breathed his last—how could she know *anything* about the Dalton case?"

"She didn't get it from me," Emmitt said, "but she knows. She told me to tell you something else too."

"Well, spit it out," Graham said, taking another sip of his coffee.

"She told me to tell you that the Dalton case was tried in the Felix County Courthouse."

Graham sputtered into his drink and nearly choked. Emmett gave him a few healthy claps on the back, and then immediately apologized for the coffee he caused Graham to spill on his shirt and coat in his overenthusiasm. Graham waved him off and attempted to brush away the amber beads of liquid before they had a chance to soak into his uniform. He was partially successful. Emmett grabbed a nearby napkin and handed it to him.

"Much obliged," Graham coughed, still struggling to clear his throat.

"What does that mean, Graham?" Emmett asked once he was sure his boss had recovered. "The Dalton case wasn't tried at all, and there is no Felix County in Georgia. I checked. There's a township in Illinois by that name, and an unincorporated community in California, but that's about it."

"You're absolutely sure that's what she said?" Graham demanded.

Emmett nodded. "Sure as I'm standing here."

Graham and Emmett returned their attention to the lone occupant of the small room. The child inside continued to scribble, seemingly oblivious to their existence. The two men stood silent and still for a long moment, a testament to how troubled they both were by the presence of their young visitor.

"She wouldn't tell me why she was here, beyond wanting to speak to you of course," Emmett eventually said without taking his eyes off the girl. "But she did say that it was a matter of life or death."

2

Graham entered his makeshift interrogation room after making it clear to Emmett he needed complete privacy. This meant that everyone, including Emmett himself, should stay the hell away. Graham knew that this decision was unwise, particularly in a day and age where acts and accusations of sexual misconduct between adults and children were rampant, but he didn't want his conversation with the child to be overheard.

It was the Felix County Court comment that bothered him most. He could explain away how the girl might have known all the other things, but there was absolutely no way she could have known about Felix County Court. While he had failed to hide his initial shock from his deputy, he thought he had successfully masked how deeply distressed he had actually been by the girl's statement. As he approached the table, he did his best to present an air of genial indifference, but distressed or not, he intended to get an explanation from her, one way or another.

"Alright little lady," he grumbled, dropping himself into

the seat opposite the child. "What's this big emergency of yours?"

The girl scribbled one last sentence on her final blank sheet of paper, before placing the completed pile in a neat stack, business side down, in front of her. She slowly spun the stack to face her host, and then, without speaking, she turned the first sheet of paper over and placed it to the right of the pile. Scrawled in impeccably neat penmanship, Graham read:

Alright little lady. What's this big emergency of yours?

It took Graham a moment to realize that the words written on the paper were the exact words he had just spoken. "Well, that's a neat trick," Graham said, sipping his coffee. "Wanna tell me how ya did it?"

The girl waited a few seconds after Graham stopped speaking as if she wanted to be sure he had nothing else to add. She then turned the next sheet of paper over and placed it on top of the first. It read:

Well, that's a neat trick. Wanna tell me how ya did it?

Graham frowned as a shiver of unease made its way down his back like a trail of cold sweat. After clearing his throat in an attempt to bolster what little composure he had, he said, "Okay look. If this little game is all you came for, there are much more important things I could be doing."

Appearing completely unintimidated by the sheriff's sour disposition, the girl calmly took the next sheet of paper from the larger stack, turned it over and placed it on top of the smaller stack. It read:

Okay look. If this little game is all you came for, there are much more important things I could be doing.

Graham folded his arms in annoyance, leaned back in his chair and sat glaring at the girl. She returned his stare, displaying no emotion, but she did occasionally glance at her wristwatch. Eventually, she turned over the top sheet of the first stack and placed it on the second. It read:

A full minute has passed, and you just sat there looking at me.

Graham's scowl deepened, but he remained silent. When another timed eternity passed in the same manner, the girl flipped the next sheet. It read:

Another full minute has passed, and you just sat there looking at me.

In a stint of stubborn defiance, the likes of which had earned him the unflattering moniker of "mule" from his closest acquaintances (he had no real friends), Graham remained silent and unflinching. When yet another full minute passed according to her wristwatch, the girl turned the next sheet. It read:

A third full minute has passed, and you just sat there looking at me, Mule.

Growling in disgust, Graham reached over and grabbed the top sheet of the unread stack. He flipped it over. It read:

You grabbed this sheet of paper and turned it over.

A tinge of worry slowly etched itself onto Graham's brow,

and his resolve visibly faltered. His mind suddenly made an involuntary connection to an earlier thought. *Something is really wrong here.* Wasn't that what he had said about the town? Could this girl be the wrongness he had sensed? Surely not. *She's just a child after all. A creepy… psychic… grifter child.* He shook his head to dispel this ridiculous notion and flipped the next sheet over. It read:

You also grabbed this sheet and turned it over.

Thinking he could beat her at this game, because surely this could be nothing other than a game, Graham angrily grabbed several sheets at once. The girl remained motionless, watching him intently. Holding the papers he had grabbed in his right hand, Graham flipped rapidly through them with his left. The first read:

This is the first of seven sheets you grabbed all at once.

The next read:

This is the second sheet of seven.

And…

This is the third sheet of seven.

Graham stopped after reading, *This is the fifth sheet of seven.* He could see that the next one in his hand read, *This is the sixth sheet of seven, and you're wondering what will happen if you ask me to move it and expose the seventh underneath.* The statement on the page mirrored his thoughts exactly, but how on earth could that be? How was she doing this? Or more precisely, how had she done this? The girl, who had remained emotionless through this silent spectacle, just stared at him. Graham set the two remaining sheets down on the table and slowly pushed them toward the girl. She reached for the sixth one, seemingly intent on exposing the seventh, but Graham held up a hand to stop her. After a moment of thought, he turned the sixth over himself. The one below read:

This is the seventh sheet. You decided to move the sixth yourself.

Graham's eyes locked on those cryptic words, and he found himself unable to turn away. He didn't realize his hand was quivering uncontrollably until the girl reached across the table to still his with her own. Considering how he felt at that moment, it was a credit to the sheriff that he managed not to snatch his hand away. In a light and compassionate voice, which seemed to offer all the mercy she must have been withholding during this ordeal, the girl said, "I think you're ready to hear my story now."

3

My name is Naomi," the girl said. "I'm a middle-school student at Heaton Academy. I'm not psychic, I can't read minds, and I'm not a hacker or a con artist. I know the things I know because this isn't the first time we've met."

Graham looked doubtful. "I don't remember ever having met any middle-schoolers from Heaton named Naomi."

"You never do," Naomi said with a mirthless chuckle.

"I never do?" Graham asked, frowning. "What do you mean, I never do?"

"You never remember me," she replied sadly.

"You're gonna have to be a little more clear if you expect me to keep up," Graham remarked. "I'm not as young as I used to be."

"I know," she said, and as if sensing that her remark might be misunderstood, she quickly added, "About me being clearer, not about your age." She paused for a moment as if waiting for Graham to comment. When he failed to, she sighed heavily. "Okay here goes." Gesturing to the room at large, she said. "This isn't the first time we've done this.

We've had this exact same conversation, in this exact same spot, hundreds, maybe even thousands of times before."

"Uh huh," Graham grunted. His patience was obviously wearing thin, but his level of irritation had not yet eclipsed his curiosity.

Naomi took a deep breath, and opened her mouth as though to speak, then paused and let it out. She took another breath and started to speak again, then sighed. Seeing the girl's difficulty made Graham feel a slight touch of compassion for her, but he balanced it by reminding himself that something wasn't quite right here, and that lack of rightness needed to be cleared up. *Yes, she's a child,* he thought, *but even children can be taught to run a scam.* He knew it was best to remain as open-minded as possible, which would be no small feat on his part, but he also planned to hold firmly to his skepticism.

"Our town... no, our world... I guess maybe even our entire universe, is stuck in a time loop, Graham," Naomi finally managed to say. "We're reliving the same hours of the same day over and over and over again, without end." At this statement, tears began to roll down her cheeks, and for the first time, Graham noted the utterly exhausted look on the child's face. He sympathized, but his rational policeman's mind wouldn't allow for this kind of nonsense.

"Groundhog Day?" he suggested, somewhat cynically.

"You call it that," she said, nodding. "You sometimes even call it 'Shadow Play,' which you said was an old *Twilight Zone* episode with a similar premise."

Graham attempted to offer her a compassionate smile, but he was sure she probably read it as a condescending sneer. He couldn't detect any untruthfulness in her manner, so he concluded that the child was confused, or perhaps not quite right in the head. Either way, it was time for this foolishness to end. "I'm sorry, Miss...?"

"Naomi," she sighed.

"Naomi what?" Graham prompted.

"Just Naomi," she insisted. "And you're just Graham. The faster we both accept that, the better things will be."

"Okay, Naomi," he conceded, desperately wanting to get past this so he could go home and get some well-deserved rest. "I can see that you're upset, but you don't really expect me to believe what you just said, do you?"

With an impatient and tearful shake of her head, Naomi turned over the next sheet of paper. It read:

Okay, Naomi. I can see that you're upset, but you don't really expect me to believe what you just said, do you?

When she was certain he had finished reading, she added, "Yes Graham, I do."

"If I turn over the next sheet of paper," Graham said. "Is it going to say, 'You grabbed this sheet of paper'?"

She fixed him with a gaze that expressed far more wisdom than her young face should have been able to muster, and said, "It will read the same thing it has read hundreds of times before."

"Which is?" he asked.

"Exactly what you need to see to help you believe me," she answered.

Looking extremely doubtful, Graham reached over and flipped the page. It read:

You know there's only one way that I could possibly know about both the Dalton case and the Court of Felix County.

He didn't realize how spooked he had been by those words until he saw a little honey toned hand reach across the table for the second time and touch his own. Graham flinched slightly, but again he successfully avoided snatching his hand away. He frowned a question in the child's direction. Her answer to his unspoken inquiry was given in a way he could truly appreciate. In fact, he wished most answers in life could come to him in the exact same way–short, to the point, and unquestionably accurate.

She said, "You told me."

4

G raham reluctantly agreed to do what Naomi asked, which meant leaving the precinct immediately on an errand of her choosing, but he had one condition. Before stating that condition, he searched his parka for his handkerchief, to wipe away an errant bead of coffee he had failed to notice earlier. When he found his pockets empty, he remembered that his handkerchief was elsewhere.

"Wrapped around the raven in your trunk," Naomi pointed out with a knowing grin. "What did it say this time? Three six four seven something?"

"Three six five three twelve, or twelfth," Graham muttered. "How…," he began, but then stopped once he thought better of it.

"Not exactly sure what it means by that," she admitted. "I know it's not an address though, because some of the numbers change."

He was on the verge of suggesting that maybe the raven was counting the number of times it had hit his car, the full implications of which were truly unsettling, when he realized that doing so would mean he was buying in to this girl's crazy notions. "How 'bout you just tell me what you know about the Dalton case and Felix County," he demanded. "And it better be good or we aren't going anywhere."

"Well, I guess I better start with Jasper Dalton then," Naomi said, glancing at her wristwatch again. The timepiece depicted a cartoonish drawing of a feline that Graham now recognized as Hello Kitty, with the red-sleeved arm of her dress representing the hour hand, and the blue-sleeved arm representing the minute hand. "But please don't interrupt any more than you absolutely have to, ok?" she bade him.

"I'll hold my tongue 'til the end," he said.

"You won't," she said with a smirk. "You always say that, but you never do."

"Alright," he said, waving impatiently. "Get started."

"Jasper Lee Dalton, according to you, was a royal pain in the ass and a first-class sack of white trash shit." Seeing Graham's scowl concerning her use of profanity, Naomi added, "Sorry. Anywho, Jasper had been in and out of trouble with his mentally deficient hillbilly parents—those are your words, not mine—with his criminally inept teachers—again, your words—and with the local law…a group whom you oddly had no deprecating adjectives for."

She paused and grinned as if waiting for a reaction, apparently believing she had managed to say something clever. When no reaction came, she cleared her throat, mumbled something about a tough crowd, and continued. "That was how life was with him as far back as anyone knowing him could recall, and according to you, the whole town knew how things with him would eventually end. The only question in everyone's mind was, would whatever he did to land himself in prison be a victimless crime, or would some poor innocent person pay for Jasper's ticket to a life of incarceration.

"Unfortunately, it ended up being the latter. Unbeknownst to everyone, Jasper gained a sick fondness for a poor girl much, much younger than he. She was younger even than me, according to you. He kidnapped her one day while she was on her way home from school, and he probably had something even more horrific in mind for her than what ended up happening. The problem was, that little girl was a fighter who didn't appreciate being abducted, and she never considered what might happen to her if she stabbed an unstable first-class sack of white trash shit in the eye with a pencil when he tried to kiss her. Other than that, all you've ever told me about little Hailey Finch was that she was a lovely strawberry-blond child, that she had been adored by her parents, and that you never found all the pieces of her. You did find her head though, and you said that if you live another hundred years, you'll never forget the look on her tiny face."

"My God, that poor baby," Graham whispered, shaking his head in both anger and disgust. "What her last moments must have been…"

Looking truly sympathetic, Naomi flipped the top sheet of her much-diminished stack of paper. On it Graham read:

My God, that poor baby. What her last moments must have been…

She then quickly flipped the next. It read:

Sorry, but I told you you'd interrupt.

He nodded and motioned for her to continue.

"You found Jasper pretty quickly," she said, "which probably had something to do with him not being in any way a criminal genius."

"Lord, ain't *that* the truth," Graham muttered.

"Jasper, who you said was a sobbing mess, confessed to everything," she continued. "Not that he needed to. He neglected to change clothes, and the idiot was literally covered in his victim's blood, not to mention his own. This, unfortunately, ended up working to his advantage because Emmett, revolted by Jasper's appearance, did a poor job handcuffing him. Long story short, he escaped and a manhunt ensued. Your three regrets, none of which according to you are the kind you lose sleep over, were as follows."

She ticked off her statements by tapping three of her fingers as she voiced each one.

"First, that you allowed the victim's father, who happened to be an experienced tracker, to join the search. Second, that you took the father's hunting rifle from him, but you let him keep his hunting knife. And third, that you decided to follow the inexperienced dogs you had with you, even after you noticed the father glancing off in another direction. The father eventually left the group, telling you he wanted to go home and comfort his wife, but you were pretty sure he intended to do no such thing. You only ever found pieces of Jasper too, and while you did later question the father, no one was ever arrested, or even investigated, for Jasper's murder."

"Whoever it was saved us the trouble of a trial," Graham said, shrugging unapologetically.

"Right. So, can we leave now?" Naomi asked.

"Where is it you want to go so badly?" he inquired.

"I can't tell you yet," she said.

"Why?"

"Because you still don't believe me."

"Maybe I do," he offered.

"You don't," she stated flatly. "You're getting there, but you still have doubts."

"Alright," he sighed. "You seem to have Jasper Dalton covered, so I guess you better tell me about Felix County court."

"Sure thing," she said. "But first you need to tell Emmett, no."

He looked confused. "Come again?"

Naomi flipped the next sheet on her stack, after which there appeared to be only one sheet remaining. The new sheet read:

Sorry to interrupt, Graham, but do either of you want anything? I'm running across the street to the Stop and Snack.

Graham was startled from his reading by a knock at the door. He inwardly reproached himself for being so skittish, thinking, *Pull yourself together dammit. Didn't the kid just give you a heads up?* He barked an irritated, "Yeah," at the door, and Emmett let himself in.

"Sorry to interrupt, Graham," Emmett muttered, "but do either of you want anything? I'm running across the street to the Stop and Snack."

There were several seconds of pregnant silence which Graham spent staring at the sheet of paper bearing Emmett's exact words. "No," he eventually said. "We're good."

Emmett, who had also been staring at the paper, nodded once, looking somewhat stricken, and then quietly shut the door.

"Felix County court," Graham said, grabbing the edge of the table as if he needed its help to stay grounded in reality. "Let's hear it while I'm still sane."

"There was this married guy," Naomi began. "You said that his name isn't important, so let's just call him John Doe. Anywho, John became recently wealthy by unexpectedly making partner in a very prestigious law firm. Soon after his promotion, John filed for divorce from his wife of seven years—let's call her Jane Doe, who coincidently had just received a diagnosis of a particularly nasty type of cancer.

"Shortly after the divorce, John got engaged to his younger, prettier, healthier, and blonder secretary, who shall remain nameless. He offered shared custody of their beautiful twin boys, telling Jane he was not only willing to pay her a healthy alimony uncontested, but that he would also let her keep the family home if she wanted to stay there. He was also willing to bear the financial responsibility for her ever-growing medical bills.

"A distraught Jane managed to convince a judge that John left her because she got sick, and that he had been verbally and physically abusive to her throughout the marriage. She also claimed John had been having an affair with the prettier blonder secretary for years, and that he never wanted children anyway, so she should get sole custody of the boys. To counter this, John alleged that Jane, a little mouse of a woman, was actually the one that had been verbally and physically abusive in the marriage, and that the abuse was the reason he had been planning to leave her, a decision which he made long before he knew she was sick. He admitted to not wanting children but said that he only felt that way because their marriage was going so poorly. He also admitted to finding comfort in the conversations he had with his secretary about his unhappiness but claimed that there was no affair.

"Jane won everything John offered as well as sole custody of the twins. Three days later she drowned the three-year-old boys in the bathtub and then slit her wrists and climbed in next to them. Near their bodies, the police found a handwritten note that made it clear that John had been telling the truth about everything, and that Jane had done what she had done purely out of vengeance and spite."

Naomi paused a moment, either to allow what she had said to sink in, or to be certain Graham was still paying attention. When he waved his hand indicating she should get on with it, she continued.

"This sad story is actually a true one. The events took place in Los Angeles, California, but you tell yourself that the outcome would have been no different, and those poor boys would have been just as dead if it had been a case held in Felix County court, because just like everyone else, you believed Jane and you damned John. You've held on to that story to remind yourself that things are not always as they seem. Most people don't know it, but Felix is your middle name. Felix County court is imaginary, and it only takes place in your head."

5

As instructed by the girl who had assumed leadership of their motley two-person crew, they exited out the back door of the precinct, into the gated lot where several impounded vehicles were being stored.

"That's the one we need to take," Naomi said, pointing to an aged Buick that had been seized in an unusually violent drug bust a month earlier. "Any other would be a problem, including your personal."

Dubbed "Old Puke Green" by Graham during a rare bout of mirth, the Riviera had been riddled with bullet holes during the raid, but had by some miracle remained drivable, and had only lost a single back window. The other windows were so heavily (and illegally) tinted that anyone trying to look inside from the outside would only see human-shaped shadows. It had already been scoured for potential evidence, and the broken glass had long ago been collected from the backseat. A discussion had come up about it being useful as an undercover vehicle, and pursuant to that, frosted plastic had been duct-taped over the gaping hole. It was no one's definition of pretty, but it could get them where they needed to go in relative comfort, so the sheriff didn't argue.

"Okay," Graham said, taking another sip of his coffee. "Wait here while I go fetch the keys."

Naomi held out her hand, inside which were a pair of car keys, attached to a brown leather keychain in the shape of dog poo, inscribed with the words, *Let it never be said that I didn't give a shit.*

"I won't ask how you got those," Graham muttered, taking the keys.

"Good," Naomi said, smiling. "Because you wouldn't approve."

Without responding, Graham headed toward the exit gate, which was padlocked shut, and Naomi headed toward the Buick. He unlocked the gate while she waited patiently near the passenger side door. After pulling the gate open wide, he joined her, unlocked her door, and opened it for her.

"Muchos grassy ass," she chirped, before tossing in her backpack and then climbing in after it. "You get it?" she asked with a giggle from inside. "Grassy ass instead of graci–" Naomi's words were cut off when Graham shut the door in her face. When he let himself into the car, he noted her disappointed glare. Ignoring her, he buckled his seatbelt and started the car. "I'd ask who peed in your cornflakes this morning," she said as he backed away from the building, "but I already know you haven't had a chance to get any breakfast or any sleep and are in an exceptionally grumpy mood."

Graham was about to tell her she was one hundred ten percent correct, when for the second time today (and in as many cars) he was forced to slam on his brakes.

"What the hell!" he exclaimed.

His words caused Naomi, who was buckling her seat-belt, to follow his gaze. When she saw what had grabbed his attention, she let out an exclamation of her own. Standing on the sidewalk just outside of the opened gate stood the broken faced clown child and the scarred albino dog.

"Holy shit!" Naomi said.

"Watch your mouth!" Graham growled.

"But it's too soon for this to be happening," Naomi said, seemingly more to herself than to him. "This isn't supposed to happen here…"

"Are you saying you know that kid?" Graham asked.

"Well, not really… but," Naomi began, obviously disturbed. After a moment of contemplation, she said, "If they don't move, you have to run them down, Graham."

"What?" Graham nearly shouted, making no attempt to hide his shock. "You mean hit the kid?"

"Yes!" Naomi insisted. "And the creepy ass dog too, if you can!"

"You have officially lost your mind," Graham said. "And I'm putting a stop to this nonsense before someone gets hurt." He put the car in park, unbuckled his seatbelt, and turned to open the door, but paused when he felt a tiny hand grasp his arm.

"Please don't go out there, Graham!" Naomi begged. "I know you're still having trouble believing me, but I swear to you that if you confront that thing right now, you're going to die, and when they're done with you, they'll come after me, which means I'll have to start all over when the day resets tomorrow, which won't really be tomorrow. It'll just be today all over again."

"You know that sounds insane, right?" he said.

"I do," Naomi agreed. "Believe me, I do, but if you give me the chance, I'll prove to you I'm telling the truth."

Graham felt himself giving in to his companion's words. He also felt disgusted with himself. He turned to stare at

Naomi, and in her pleading watery eyes he saw sincerity. Still, he hesitated.

"This is your chance to fix things before it's too late," she said, "rather than picking up the pieces afterward. A chance to do something that truly matters."

Recognizing his own thoughts coming from the girl's mouth, he sighed, buckled his seatbelt, and then shifted the gear from P to D as a declaration of his decision. "I'm not going to hit the kid though," he stated flatly, as he started forward. "Or the creepy ass dog."

"Okay," Naomi said, nodding. "Thank you for believing me."

With a noncommittal grunt, he honked the horn, hoping it would be enough to clear their way forward. It wasn't. The unexpected sounds emanating from the hood were identical to those made by the Dodge Charger bearing the name "General Lee" from the television show The Dukes of Hazzard. Hearing a horned rendition of "oh I wish I was in the land of cotton," might have been laughable in other situations, but it only added to the growing tension as Graham edged the car past the child/clown and her monster dog. Both stared menacingly into the vehicle as it passed, and Graham found himself feeling thankful for those excessively dark tinted windows. He wasn't certain, but he thought he heard the dog's low growl while it was inches away from his door. He was, however, very certain he heard the passenger side door scrape against the gate as he slowly squeezed the Buick through the space left between it, the child, and the dog. He more than half expected the albino beast to burst through the plastic covering the back window and released a breath which he hadn't realized he had been holding when they finally reached the main road. Through the back window, he could see both the dog and the child apparently glaring at them as they drove away. He briefly turned to Naomi, who had been silent and still throughout the ordeal, and noted that she looked just as wide eyed and frightened as he would never admit to being. Probably even more so.

"You know," Graham said, in a tone obviously meant to ease the tension. "I've heard that same horn go off a hundred times or more on that hillbilly show, and it took me being in this car with you now to make me realize how racist all of that was."

Naomi turned to him with a smile that quavered slightly around the edges, seemingly comforted by the kindness in his voice. "What show?"

Graham shook his head and grinned.

Once they were several blocks away from the precinct, Graham realized he had no idea where she wanted him to go.

"Where are we headed," he asked, as he attempted to coax the Buick's ancient heater to life. It sputtered for a moment and then died, but not before coughing a few spore-laden clouds of dust through the vents, forcing the pair to crack their windows to rid Old Puke Green of its meth lab mildew stench, and leaving him thankful that they were both wearing thick parkas.

"To the South Reverie Glen neighborhood, please," Naomi said, as she began to rummage through her backpack.

Glancing over, Graham noted that the pack bore another depiction of Hello Kitty, making it a coordinating accessory with the girl's watch. "I half expected you to say, and step on it," he muttered.

"No need," Naomi replied, shaking her head. "We've got a little time, but could you throw out your coffee please?"

Graham briefly turned to the cupholder which separated the driver's seat from the passenger's, and he was surprised to find it occupied by the cup that Emmett had given him. He couldn't recall putting it there, but he must have because there it was. Forgetfulness aside, he was thankful, because the cinnamon-hued liquid within was all that kept him going at this point. "Why?" he asked, retrieving the cup and taking a large mouthful, which was only possible because it had cooled considerably. "Having it gonna cause some kinda problem somewhere in the future or something?"

"No," she admitted. "But you're going to be tempted to drink it every so often, and you driving with one hand makes me nervous."

"Alright," he said, taking one final gulp of the tepid brown fluid. He stopped the car, opened the door, and poured the remainder on the ground, prompting Naomi to turn and take a nervous glance out the back window.

"In a bad horror movie, the dog would have been right there waiting for you," she said somewhat nervously, as he pulled the door shut.

"Then let's be glad we aren't in a bad horror movie," he said, as he first crumpled and then tossed the empty cup into the backseat.

"Don't be so sure," she said, returning to her exploratory task.

He considered questioning that statement, thought better of it, and got the car moving again. "Are we headed to a specific house in Reverie?" he asked.

She nodded. "1999 Pensive Drive."

"1999 Pensive," he echoed. "I think I might know that house."

"You do," she said, pulling two books from her bag. "But that's not important right now. There are a few things we need to go over before we get there, okay? Important things."

"Alright," he said, turning onto a new street. A frown creased his brow as it occurred to him that he had not bothered leaving a note for Emmett. As soon as his deputy realized he and the girl were gone and the Buick was missing, he would worry. Graham was reaching for his walkie-talkie when Naomi chimed in.

"Don't worry about Emmett," she said. "I left him a note."

He turned his frown on her, though it was now expressing curiosity rather than concern. It softened a bit when he remembered the last piece of paper on the table that had remained unturned.

"What did it say," he asked.

"That we were leaving in the Buick, and that he knows he can trust you," she said. "But turn off your walkie-talkie just the same."

"Emmett's gonna interrupt at some inconvenient moment if I don't?" he asked, shifting his bulk to one side with a grunt. This was necessary to reach the knob on the walkie.

"You're a fast learner," Naomi said, smiling. "That's why we get along so well." She held up one of the books she retrieved from her bag. It was large and black, and the title on it read, *A Spiral of Depravity*. "Ever read this?" she asked.

After a quick glance at the title, Graham cut his eyes at her in answer.

"Okay, I know you haven't," she admitted. "Anywho, it was written by a woman named Melinoë. She has published a bunch of books where she writes about humanity's shortcomings, and they all have the word 'spiral' in the title. There's one called *A Spiral of Foreboding*, where she claims that most of the decisions we make day to day are based on our fears rather than our hopes, and there's another called *A Spiral of Insincerity*, where she claims that most of us lie or exaggerate more often than we tell the truth."

Naomi paused long enough to give the book she held a brief shake before continuing.

"In the first half of this one, she explains her research

methods and how it brought her to the conclusion that there are, at any given time, somewhere around thirty or more active cults in the United States whose beliefs advocate, and sometimes even demand, violence against nonbelievers. She defined nonbelievers as generally anybody the cult members disagree with, unless of course, they're in a recruiting kind of mood. She also said that the ones she is referring to as 'cult members' don't have to necessarily know one another, and that it's possible for these cults to just be a group of broken and dispirited strangers who happen to have like-minded sentiments. People like that can end up working toward a common goal without even realizing it. According to Melinoë, these cults thrive in small out-of-the-way towns like this one. When they're organized, they tend to be cautious, biding their time while gradually building their power and influence in the area until they can spread their agenda of fear and terror. When they're unorganized, they tend to haphazardly prey on drifters and vagrants, while unknowingly maintaining a general air of wrongness. Still with me?"

Graham nodded. "Murder cults. Small towns. Agendas of fear and terror. Gotcha."

"Good. So, all this stuff about cults leads to what Ms. Melinoë calls a 'Spiral of Depravity,'" Naomi said, gesturing to the book. "Thus, the title. It's around the middle of the book where her beliefs take a bit of a supernatural turn. She says that when particularly horrible things happen consistently in a given area, it taints the region with a kind of spiritual malevolence. She believes that some people can actually sense this malevolence, and the ones she interviewed are quoted in the book as saying it feels like a general air of wrongness around them, or something like that."

Graham shot Naomi a quick glance and saw that she was staring at him knowingly, and there was a notable pause in her words before she continued.

"The spiritual malevolence she writes about can supposedly attract new broken and dispirited individuals to the area, though they have no idea why they came or what makes the area so enticing to them. These people either join a local malevolent group or create a brand new one, but sometimes they act alone. Regardless, when they commit more horrible acts, they spread the taint."

"Is that where the 'Spiral' comes from in her titles?" Graham asked. "As in, 'things are spiraling out of control?'"

"Exactly," Naomi agreed. "And according to Ms. Melinoë, spirals like the one of Depravity can eventually grow to encompass entire cities, reaching the point where the allure of the taint becomes more like a calling, bringing people of ever-increasing evil intent. She says that the cycles of violence might wax or wain over time, but they never fade completely. The examples she gives are cities like Las Vegas, New York, and Chicago."

"Sounds a bit far-fetched," Graham observed, "But I guess it fits those places."

"So much more than you know," Naomi remarked, pointing out the names of the cities represented by glossy illustrations on the inner pages of the book. "She also mentions Sodom and Gomorrah, Ancient Rome, and most of the areas surrounding Auschwitz and Dachau." Having made those points, Naomi snapped the book shut, exclaiming, "That sets the tone for what's next!" After returning *A Spiral of Depravity* to her bag, she picked up the second of the two books and opened it on her lap. This one turned out to be a sketchbook/journal, and she had to flip past several well-written pages before she came to an unused one. After fishing a pen from her bag, she used it to tap on the blank page. "Imagine this is the bottom portion of Harborage County," she said. "The part below Lake Evelyn."

"Below Lake Evie," Graham agreed, nodding. "Got it."

After indicating a place near the top of the page, she said, "I'm not going to, but if I were to put a mark here, it would represent the place where I wake up every morning, on my back, in the woods, alone, when this crazy endless day begins."

"You wake up on the ground in the woods?" Graham asked.

"Well, there aren't any beds out there," Naomi pointed out. "So yeah, on the ground."

"Course," he agreed. "Sorry for interrupting."

"No problem," Naomi said, as she drew a circle on the page. "This area represents the furthest I can get in any given direction if I do nothing but walk until my time runs out, which incidentally, is at midnight."

"This all is just so insane," Graham remarked.

"I agree," Naomi said. "But it's happening. And in case you were wondering, the reason why my starting spot isn't in the middle of the circle is because some places are harder to get through than others, like the Elder Hollow. That forest is impossible to get through. Scary too, so when I go in the opposite direction, I get farther."

Graham nodded but remained silent while trying to decide exactly how far he should allow this to go before he decided to put his foot down. He had already allowed this girl to charm him into going along with her delusion, mostly because he couldn't figure out how she knew what she knew, though now he included the slight possibility that he might unearth answers to the wrongness of the town by locating more pieces to his puzzle, but there was a point when enough was enough.

"I've searched pretty much the entire inside of this circle," she said with a sigh. "There's some truly weird and frightening stuff tucked away here and there, but nothing that really mattered. So, then I started exploring the edges of the circle, and that's when I discovered something interesting."

"What's that?" he asked.

"That some places have pumpkins," she responded.

"Congratulations," he said with a laugh. "You've discovered something that half the town already knew."

"Half the town knows that some places have jack-o'-lanterns," she pointed out. "The places I'm talking about have a pumpkin. Or to be more specific, they have a single, perfect, uncarved pumpkin, growing right out of the ground."

"Impossible," he said. "It's too late in the year, and too cold."

"You're right," she agreed. "They shouldn't be able to grow in this snowy weather, but they're there just the same." After a moment of consideration, she added, "Of course, that doesn't explain why those jack-o'-lanterns all around town aren't rotting."

"And where exactly are these magical pumpkins growing?" he asked, making no attempt to mask his sarcasm.

"Well," she began, as she slid her finger back and forth across an area outside the circle's upper portion. "If I pointed out that the Elder Hollow Forest is here, what would you say is here on the left side of the circle?" Before he could answer, in a tone of self-reproach, she said, "Actually, let's call it the *West* side of the circle instead of the *left* side, since we're pretty much making a map here, okay?"

Graham nodded. "Okay."

"So, did anything out of the ordinary happen in that general area recently?"

"Depends on what you mean by recently," Graham replied after taking a quick peek at the drawing.

"Within the last five years or so," Naomi said.

"I may have scolded a few jaywalkers somewhere around–"

"Graham…" Naomi interjected, cutting her eyes at him.

"The Rising Star Daycare poisonings," Graham said somberly. "One of the most disturbing things I've ever seen. A carbon monoxide leak from the building's natural gas powered hot-water heater. They didn't realize they were breathing it in until it was too late. Twelve victims total." He paused for a moment before adding, "… nine of 'em were toddlers. When the owner was told what happened, she had a nervous breakdown and later took her own life out of guilt and shame, believing she had been responsible by neglecting to do some kind of maintenance on the thing. She was wrong though. Our investigation proved that the water heater had been tampered with, making it a mass homicide, but discovering that didn't get us any closer to finding out who did it. We still don't know to this day." With a sideways glance at his passenger, he added, "You couldn't have been more than eight or so when that happened, so how on earth would you even…" He stopped speaking after seeing the exasperated look she was giving him.

"Moving on," she said and marked another place on the opposite edge of the circle. "What about here, on the East side near Beggers Rock?"

Graham took another peek. "Same general time frame?"

Naomi shook her head. "A little bit closer to the present."

"That would probably be the fifty or so animal carcasses we found in the woods."

"And how did you find them?" she asked.

"Some kids playing nearby smelled–"

"No," she interrupted. "I don't mean what led you to them. I mean how were they arranged."

"Is that really necessary," Graham asked, while slowly turning the car onto a new street.

"Yes," Naomi insisted. "It is."

Graham cut his eyes at her, looking as reluctant to answer as he felt. "I don't think it's a good idea to discuss these kinds of things with a minor."

"I already know the answer, Graham," she reminded him. "Not only have you told me this before, but I've been there."

"You've *been* there?" he asked, incredulous.

"Yup," she responded, in a tone far too lighthearted for the current conversation. "At night even, and boy oh boy was that terrifying."

"But we had that area blocked off!" he insisted.

"And since when has yellow tape or warning signs ever stopped anyone?" she chuckled.

"Why on earth would you go there?" he asked in the tone of a scolding parent. "The place smells worse than a landfill, and there are still pieces of dead critters rotting in the branches."

"To save the world from this craziness," Naomi said with an audible tremble in her voice, sounding more like a weary child than she had since this all began. Graham stole a glance at her and saw tears welling up in her eyes. "All of this," she sighed, waving her arms around in general. "The whole point of everything we're doing now, and everything I've done before, is to bring a final end to this awful God damned day."

"Watch your mouth," Graham growled, before adding in a more apologetic tone, "But okay. I understand."

"We have to set things right soon, Graham," Naomi sniffed, "because I don't think I can do this much longer."

"How about you finish your map," Graham suggested, "and I'll try to stick to just answering your questions."

"Okay," she sniffed, wiping her cheeks with her sleeve. "Sorry. I thought I was past moments like that." She cleared her throat and then said, "So, the animals–dogs, cats, pigs…

even deer–were gutted and strung up in the trees by their necks or their legs. Some of them were even skinned."

"Yeah," Graham grudgingly admitted, giving a grim nod.

"Now if I make a mark here at the very bottom…"

"That would be about where we are headed now," he said. "South Reverie Glen."

"Yes, and the last two places with pumpkins would be here and here," she said, marking two spots slightly apart from one another at the top of the circle. Touching the west most of the top two dots, she asked, "Anything here?"

"That would be the mass grave those contractors dug up while they were clearing the land for a new housing development," he said. "The history folks from Holme University say it's the biggest they've ever seen and is likely slaves caught and murdered after a failed rebellion or escape attempt."

"Exactly," she agreed. "Which leaves this one," she said in a tone of reluctance, tapping the final spot.

Graham briefly glanced at her work.

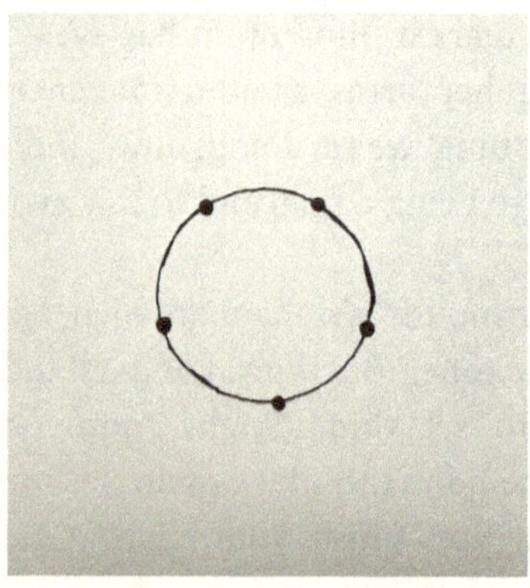

"There's nothing special there," he said, pulling the car to a stop at the curb. "Just old farmland and acres of deep woods. We're here, by the way. 1999 is that three-story faded pink Victorian with the wrap-around porch."

"Good," she said. "It's best if you turn the car off now."

He did so, after putting it in park, and then turned to face her fully.

"We should have a few more minutes to talk," she said, glancing down at her watch. "Which is good because there's more that you need to know."

"Okay," he said, settling back in his seat. "Let's hear it."

Her glance drifted from his face to her lap, and she cleared her throat but didn't speak. A frown of confusion crossed Graham's brow when he realized that for the first time since their introduction, Naomi seemed to be having trouble looking him in the eyes. At first, he found it amusing, considering her forward personality thus far, but when the silent seconds grew to be uncomfortably long, his impatience intervened.

"What is it?" he prompted.

"That old farmland you mentioned," she said. "There *is* something out there."

"Something as bad as the other places?" he probed, sounding genuinely curious.

"Yeah," she said, nodding. "Pretty bad."

"And I assume there's something pretty bad here as well," he pointed out, "seeing as how you've brought us here."

Again, she nodded. "Yeah. Pretty bad."

"Okay," he said, trying to sound comforting. "Which one you wanna tell me about first?"

"This one," she said, finally turning to face him. "You're going to insist on going to see the other one for yourself after I tell you about it, but I brought us here because it's best that you learn about this one first."

"Alright then," he said. "What happened here?"

"Before I begin," she said, with a casual nod toward the side of the nearby house. "Take a look at that."

He did. There, on the ground near the porch, in plain contrast to both the stark white of the snow and the faded pink of the home, was the most perfectly shaped, bright orange globe of a pumpkin he had ever seen. It was completely unblemished, and the noonday sunlight glinting off the ice crystals clinging to it made it appear to sparkle. A gnarled and twisted stem extended from its crown and snaked its way to the ground, displaying several leaves which resembled oversized clovers. Graham stared at the seemingly unnatural gourd, utterly transfixed.

"I found one exactly like it at each of the five places I mentioned," he heard Naomi say. "And there aren't any others anywhere else in this entire part of the county."

"But why here?" he asked, his eyes still on the pumpkin.

"To mark the locations as special, maybe," she offered. He didn't need to look at her to know she had shrugged. He heard it in her voice. "But forget the pumpkin for a second," she quickly added. "Who's that coming up the sidewalk?"

Graham turned, squinted, and then remarked, "Isn't that one of the town librarians?" After a moment of mental fumbling, followed by a snap of his fingers when her name occurred to him, he said, "Clarissa, right?"

A tall, thin, bespectacled woman, whose severely austere appearance said she wasn't aware the 1960s had come and gone, was slowly making her way along the snow-covered pavement, leaving petite footprints. She clutched a tiny, tattered handbag to her meager breasts with both of her mitten-clad hands, occasionally casting nervous glances to her left and right.

"That's her," Naomi agreed.

He did not need to turn to his companion to know she

had a look of disgust on her face. He could hear it. "But it's midday," Graham remarked, dumbfounded. "That woman never misses a single day of work, and when I say *never*, I mean *never*. I hear she's so anal retentive about time, it's a running joke at the library. They say you can damn near set your watch by her."

"That's what they say," Naomi conceded, still sounding disgusted.

"1999 is her house," he said, as if realizing it for the first time.

Naomi nodded. "Yup."

He turned to his companion. "You're not about to tell me that the most reclusive, soft-spoken, mousey little woman in town has something to hide that can in any way compare to a daycare full of toddlers being poisoned, or a group of slaves being murdered and tossed into a hole?"

"I am."

"And you have proof?"

"Irrefutable."

"Well, this I just gotta hear," Graham said, shifting in his seat to make himself more comfortable. "Please, enlighten me."

Naomi took a deep breath and then began. "The first thing you should know is that Clarissa is actually her middle name. When she lived in Westchester, New York, she went by her first name, Beverly. Old Bev there was married to a wealthy stockbroker named Glen, and together they lived with their five dogs in their 2.5-million-dollar home.

"Bev's socialite days came to an abrupt end when Glen was busted in a child pornography/sex trafficking sting. The local district attorney found it difficult to believe that Bev had no idea there was a tiny prison with a camera and little shackles on the wall of a secret room in her basement, and Glen, who committed suicide rather than face public humiliation, couldn't exonerate her. She got five years in Bedford Hills Correctional Facility for Women, of which she served a very hard three. Bev, who had paid others to clean her house, cook her meals, and walk her dogs, had never worked a single day in her life. Her most strenuous daily activities had been shopping and gossiping with her snobby friends. In less than a year, she lost her freedom, her home, her husband, and her social status, as well as most of her fortune to legal fees and civil lawsuits. During a particularly brutal, umm... altercation, involving three fellow inmates and a broken broomstick, she also lost the ability to have children."

"Jesus," Graham whispered.

"Yeah," Naomi agreed. "Needless to say, the whole ordeal broke her already fragile mind. Being the only child of an older couple who passed away when she was in college, she didn't have any family to speak of, and her Social Register high society friends quickly abandoned her when the pedophile story broke. When she regained her freedom, she scraped together what was left of her life, relocated here, and adopted a new identity. She got the job in the library, and other than the night terrors and anxiety attacks she experienced, both barely held in check through daily medication, things might have been alright for her. Unfortunately, a day came when Beverly, now Clarissa, witnessed a brief exchange between a young runaway and a middle-aged well-to-do gentleman near the library. The runaway, a girl Clarissa said was probably a little older than me–"

"What do you mean 'Clarissa said'?" Graham interrupted. "Are you telling me you spoke to her about this?"

"On several disturbingly memorable occasions," Naomi said solemnly. "How else would I know all this stuff? But don't interrupt. The runaway appeared to be propositioning the man–sexual favors for enough cash to buy a bus ticket to...someplace." Naomi said that last with an indifferent wave of her hand. "I don't think Clarissa knew where for certain. Regardless, what resonated with the librarian was that this kind of entrapment must have been what enticed her poor husband into a life of depravity. The ever-increasing voices in her head began to whisper to Clarissa about the 'little sluts' and 'whoring bitches' running around seducing good, honest men." Seeing the pained look on Graham's face Naomi added, "All her words, not mine. Anywho, she eventually concluded there was only one thing that would silence the voices and give her peace."

Leaning toward her companion and speaking slowly for added emphasis, Naomi said, "Sweet, mousey little Clarissa there has kidnapped, tortured, killed, and dismembered at least two innocent teenagers. Their names are Beth and Trish. Their bodies are buried in her basement, but she keeps a bloody fingernail souvenir from each one in that locket around her neck." As if it were a side note barely worth mentioning, she shrugged and said, "She's murdered three, if you count me."

"What the hell do you mean, 'if you count me?" Graham demanded, horrified.

"I mean that Clarissa has killed me at least a hundred times now," Naomi said with a shocking lack of emotion. "I can only assume that she also dismembered me, buried me, and added one of my nails to her collection, but today doesn't have to be number one hundred and one. You can change that."

"What do you expect me to do?" he asked. "Barge in without probable cause or a warrant or anything and arrest her?"

"No," Naomi said. "I expect you to kill her."

"*What?*" Graham barked, incredulous.

"She's a murderess, Graham," Naomi said flatly. "She may not have always been one, but she's definitely one now!

There's a monster hidden beneath that hair bun. A monster that hates little girls, and this morning I poked that monster with a stick. That's why she's home early."

"Ok," Graham said in a tone that meant he had heard enough. "I think its best we head back to the station and call your…"

He paused midsentence, looking befuddled. Something disconcerting was slowly occurring to him, and though Naomi was giving him a knowing glance, she let him have a moment to think it through.

"Getting there at last?" she eventually asked. "My parents, you were going to say? You're wondering why they're just now crossing your mind? Wondering why you didn't ask about them long ago?"

"Yeah," he muttered, more to himself than to her. "…I am."

"Well unfortunately, this time I don't have an answer for you. I'm not sure why it takes you this long to think of them, though my guess would be it has something to do with you already knowing that she isn't around. My dad never was, so it's my mom I'm talking about. But she's a discussion for another time. Right now, all you need to know is that I left Clarissa a note telling her that I know all about Beth and Trish, and that she needed to meet me right here, right now, and there she is. She thinks I'm one of Beth and Trish's friends who somehow found out about their murders, and that I want to blackmail her or something. So, I'm going to go knock on her door and she's going to let me in. Seventeen minutes later I'll be dead unless you come in and stop her, and when I say stop her, I mean kill her."

"You aren't serious," he said.

"Graham, every time you don't kill her, she kills you."

He stared at the child, utterly speechless. When he finally found his voice, he asked, "I've died here before?"

"You've died here a lot, as a matter of fact," Naomi

pointed out. "And every time you did, it was because you tried to, how do you put it…'talk her down?' What you don't realize is, when she answers the door, she has a knife behind her back–the same knife she'll be using on me if you don't stop her. The few times you've successfully saved me, you banged on the door instead of knocking, you pull your gun when she tries to slam the door in your face, and you shoot her before you see the knife."

"And there's always a knife?" he asked.

"Always," she stated flatly.

"I don't know," he said, running his hand through his beard stubble, displaying his obvious misgivings. "Shooting a woman based purely on an assumpt–Hey!"

Graham's shout was a reaction to Naomi opening the car door. Prompted by his inaction, she hopped out before he could stop her.

"The more we talk about it," she said from just beyond his reach, "the more you're going to rationalize yourself into a decision that ends in me getting tortured and you getting stabbed. You already know everything you need to know. Now you have to choose." She glanced at her watch. "In about nine minutes, no matter how much I fight, I'll be shackled to a wall in her basement. Seven minutes after that she'll start cutting my fingers off, slowly and painfully I might add, unless I get her talking. If I spit in her face on the third finger, she ends it faster, which I plan on doing if it comes to that, and about Seventeen minutes from entering that house, I'll be dead. You won't remember a thing when this all resets, but I'll remember every agonizing second. Spare me that, okay? Please come in before fifteen minutes have passed and bust a cap…or how about several caps, in that crazy bitch's ass."

"There's gotta be another way," he pleaded, turning to open his own door.

"We've tried other ways," she said sadly. "And it's best if you stay in the car for now."

"But we can go to the door together!" he insisted.

Again, she shook her head. "Clarissa has a gun in the hall closet, but she only pulls it out when she sees us both at the door, and she always manages to kill one of us before she dies, because she shoots first and doesn't bother asking questions later."

Naomi shut the car door before he had the chance to offer another option. She quickly made her way to the porch of the nearby house, and after sending one last pleading look in his direction, she knocked. A moment later, the door opened, and Naomi disappeared inside.

6

T his is madness," Graham muttered, opening his door. "If all the stuff she said was true we should have brought Emmett with us for backup."

He exited the vehicle shaking his head in disgust, hitched up his pants, and then made his way to the door of 1999. As he passed the pumpkin, he noted that it wasn't as perfect and pristine as he had believed. Seen from the back, the gourd had a large festering bruise which whispered a rumor of the quality of its core. *Just like my town these past few months*, Graham reflected. But had it only been months, he wondered, or had it been longer? His immediate answer was, *I don't know*, and that would have to do for now, because he was having trouble focusing on anything other than his current task. It had been no more than seven minutes since Naomi stepped into Clarissa's (or was it Beverly's) pink Victorian lair, but Graham's patience had worn thin.

He did feel slightly uneasy about going against Naomi's plan, but if what she described was going to happen, wouldn't he be in a better position to put a stop to it if he arrived earlier? He reached up and started to knock when he remembered what Naomi said, and he banged instead.

For a long, long moment, there was no answer.

He banged more urgently.

A muffled, and perhaps flustered, female voice from beyond the door called out, "Just a second!"

A moment later, the sound of multiple bolt locks being unlatched could be heard. *Now there's an oddity*, Graham thought. *Why would a librarian need more than two locks on her door in a sleepy little town like ours? Are they for safety, or are they meant to guard a secret?*

He tried his best to shake these thoughts because he knew they would interfere with his ability to remain impartial and objective. He failed. His mind insisted on jumping back and forth between giving Clarissa the benefit of every doubt and damning her as a murderess. The door eventually opened, though only a crack. *Another oddity,* he thought. *No one does that kind of thing here. It's either open wide or not at all.* From inside, the right-side portion of a thin unassuming face appeared in the shadows beyond the door.

"Sh- Sherriff Graham." Clarissa stammered. "Good morning. Is there something wrong?"

It was the hiding as if she had come to the door indecent and opened it to a priest that made him lean more toward the belief that the girl had been right. It was also Clarissa's unsteadiness, and the out-of-place nervousness that he heard in her voice. These points of contention caused him to make a split-second decision to change what he had planned to say, and part of him despaired in the knowledge that this new path would very likely lead to violence.

"It's afternoon," Graham said, dispensing with the pleasantries. "And yeah, I'm afraid there is something wrong. I'm gonna need you to let me in, Clarissa. Or should I call you Beverly?"

And there it is, he thought, doing his best to mask his disappointment. There was the telltale sign he was trying to shock her into betraying, though much of him was hoping there was nothing to betray. Graham had been an officer long enough to recognize such clues when they surfaced, and looking for them had become second nature to him. If the name Beverly had meant nothing to Clarissa, what should have followed would have been a frown of confusion. *Who the hell is Beverly,* her reaction should have said, followed by its verbal equivalent.

But that single visible eye didn't say that.

By quickly going from being a small slit squinted against the brightness of the noonday sun to a wide circle of alarm, her eye made him certain of two things. The first was that she knew damn well who Beverly was. The second was that she hadn't expected *him* to know. With these thoughts in mind, Sheriff Graham acted.

As he drew his service revolver, Graham used his considerable bulk to shoulder his way into the house, easily tearing the chain latch from the rotting wood of the door frame and knocking Clarissa on her bony rear end. She hit the ground with tooth-rattling force and something hard and metal clattered to the floor. This offered Graham one last opportunity to test Clarissa's motives, and he decided to take it. He had been told what to expect by the child, so his attention had not been immediately drawn to the object on the floor. Instead, his eyes locked on Clarissa's face.

If she wants to live, he thought, *and if she is at all remorseful about whatever she's done, she'll leave the knife and beg me not to shoot.*

He wanted this to be the case so badly, that when Clarissa raised her hand in a gesture he thought to be submission, he actually lowered his gun. Unfortunately, this movement was a ruse. If Graham had been asked to describe the deadly scuffle that followed, he probably would have avoided the question by saying that small town law enforcers don't come equipped with the words to adequately explain such things. That Clarissa had twisted with unnatural speed…that she snatched the knife from the floor and sprung at him. Yes, that much he could have conveyed. What happened with her face, on the other hand, was difficult for him to believe, much less to describe. Any attempt he might have made, perhaps for the sake of a report he hoped never to write, might have mentioned that her change in expression was so rapid and so complete it was as if all the recognizable parts of her face had melted away. The mask replacing it was twisted and distorted by anger and hate, and nothing decent remained. Clarissa's movements were so swift they seemed bestial, and Graham barely had time to react. Had her goal been to gut him, she probably would have easily succeeded. Fortunately for him, her rage would only allow wide erratic swings, with her slicing haphazardly at the air while shrieking obscenities.

"That little bitch!" Clarissa screamed. "She seduced you! Whispered her poison in your ear! Did she tell you I was pregnant! Those prison whores killed my baby! It was all I had of my poor Glen! They owe me a life! They must pay what they owe! All filthy little bitches must pay!"

Graham was bigger, stronger, and armed, but the librarian somehow managed to drive him back against the foyer wall, where he slid down in a half crouch, half cringe, struggling to defend himself. He couldn't even manage to raise his arms enough to get a clean shot. Clarissa was swinging too wildly, and he feared one of her cuts might open an artery or something. His only chance was to angle the gun up, pull the trigger, and hope for the best.

He did, he did, and he did.

7

Though it was normally concealed behind what was known in these parts as a china cabinet, Graham had little difficulty finding the stairway that led to the basement. In her earlier nervousness and haste, Clarissa left the cabinet pushed to one side and the door beyond it wide open. After being certain his unwilling host was dead—the large bloody holes in her chest and lack of breathing attested to this, Graham made his way gingerly down the stair. His progress was slow due to his injuries, and he winced with every step, but he eventually reached the bottom where he lowered himself to sit on the stairs and take a moment of rest. Once seated, he attempted to wipe the blood from his face but was only successful in smearing it across his cheeks and forehead. After a brief glance at his hands, which were trembling uncontrollably, he looked up and took in the murderous librarian's secret den. What he saw turned his stomach.

The little illumination there was in this gloomy hollow came from a single naked bulb, which hung from a large mold-covered pipe in the center of the room. Many smaller pipes ran alongside this one, each a rusted iron vein spreading in a geometric fashion across the dank underbelly of the home. The floor beneath him was bare earth, upon which were strewn several tools whose crimson stains whispered their grisly function. In one corner, Graham noticed a pair of pliers whose tiny jaws still held the remains of their most recent duty: a single human tooth. He was silently thankful that the blood on them wasn't fresh. Crumpled in a heap against the far wall, clasped in chains forcing her hands high above her head, lay a small familiar figure. She was much filthier now than she had been, most likely from being dragged across the bare earth. Her clothes were torn in several places, and like Graham, she bore several small cuts and bruises.

This is my doing, he thought. *That child put herself through this hell to prove what she said was true, because she knew that telling me wouldn't be enough.* He felt a penetrating disgust over the whole ordeal, as well as an inner shame that he knew would haunt him for the remainder of his days.

A weak and frightened voice from across the room whimpered, "Please, oh please, let that be you, Graham."

"Yeah," he said with an agonized groan. "It's me."

"Oh, thank God," Naomi breathed. "Thank God."

After a few silent seconds of rest, Graham spoke. "Let me guess," he grunted, slowly rising to his feet. "If I knew going in that she had been pregnant when those inmates performed their broomstick abortion on her, I would have felt sorry for ole Beverly up there and hesitated instead of shooting her, right?"

Naomi nodded wearily. "Uh huh."

"Did you see what she did with the key to your shackles?" he asked.

"Her pocket," Naomi sighed. "They're always in her left hip pocket."

"Wonderful," Graham grumbled as he turned to head back up the stairs. "I'll go get them, and while I'm setting you free, you can tell me where we go from here."

"*What?*" The surprise in Naomi's voice was unmistakable.

"What part of that is confusing you?" he asked, pausing in his ascent. He did his best not to sound ill-tempered, but the pain he was feeling made it difficult.

"You don't want to go to Cody's Farm?" she asked.

He sighed heavily. "I thought that last dot on your map might be my cousin's farm." After a brief pause, he added, "…distant cousin. Haven't been there in… Lord, it has to be ten years or more. Not since a little after Kelly Ann died. She was his wife. Is it really that bad out there?"

She nodded, but with his back turned, he didn't see it, so she spoke. "Yes."

"Is it the girls?" he asked sadly.

Naomi hesitated a moment, and then said, "Yes. Sarrah and Daisy."

Hearing their names said aloud was like a punch in the gut, causing Graham to slump to sit where he was and brace himself for the answer to a question he wasn't sure he wanted answered. "Has he…been at them?"

"…yes."

"But that's not all that's wrong, is it?"

"…no."

"Spit it out then."

She rattled her chains to return his attention to the task at hand. "You think maybe you could…?"

"Did he get them… you know. I mean, have there been babies?"

"…yes."

"Jesus," he groaned. "How many?"

"Three," she said. "Two boys from Sarah. One girl from Daisy."

"Where are they?"

"Graham, I don't think–"

"Where are they?"

She stared at him for a long moment, and when she finally spoke, something in her words told him this was the first time he had ever asked her that particular question, in this particular place, at this particular time. *If I answer this question, we might be walking into unfamiliar territory from here on out,* her look seemed to say. Still, she answered.

"They're in the well, Graham," she said in a near whisper. "He broke their necks right after they were born and threw them down the dry well behind his barn. The rats have a nest down there. I know about the rats, because he didn't bother breaking *my* neck when he threw *me* down the well."

Without another word, Graham stood and slowly made his way up the stairs to retrieve the key.

8

W here to now?" Graham asked. "To end this mess, I hope."

They were once again in the old Buick, leaving Pensive Drive behind, but headed nowhere specific. Graham felt it best that they vacate their current location before any nosey neighbors decided to conduct a personal investigation prompted by the gunshots. They were both still grimacing from the injuries they had sustained, with Graham being the worse off between the two.

"Yes," Naomi replied, reaching for her journal. Glancing at the numerous blood stains on Graham's shirt, she added, "Sorry about that."

"You got nothing to apologize for," he said.

"I might," she offered meekly.

"I doubt it," he responded.

"I tried something new," she said.

"Did you now," he said, sounding genuinely curious. "What?"

"This time I spat in her face right after you banged on the door," she said. "I knew she wouldn't have enough time to retaliate, and that meant she would answer the door angry. I was hoping it would help convince you to pull your gun sooner."

"Well, she was definitely angry," he agreed. "But I think it actually may have helped."

"How?"

"She was so pissed off she never managed to get a decent swing with that knife of hers. These cuts are painful, but they're mostly superficial. How about you?"

"A few cuts here and there," she said, "but the most painful is this welt from where she punched me in the face. Do you mind pulling over here? I have something I need to show you."

He stopped the Buick on the side of the road near a lamp-post which, despite the noonday sun, was lit. After putting the car in park, Graham pulled a handkerchief from his back pocket and did his best to clean his face. He also dabbed at some of the open wounds on his hands that refused to stop oozing but paused when he noticed Naomi giving him an odd look.

"What?" he asked.

"That handkerchief," she said, sounding wary. "Where'd you get it?"

"My back pocket," he said. "Why?"

"No reason," she said, switching to a tone that sounded far too casual.

He scowled for a moment in thought, and then said, "It's supposed to be in the trunk of my car wrapped around a dead raven, isn't it?"

"Yup," she replied, nodding.

"Has this ever happened before," he asked, sounding more concerned than he meant to.

"Nope," she responded, shaking her head.

"What do you think it means?"

"I don't know," she sighed. "Nothing good, I'm sure."

"We'll add it to the list then," he chuckled and then went back to tending to his wounds.

Naomi didn't interrupt again until he seemed content with his work, after which she brought his attention to the sketchbook on her lap by tapping it with her pen. He noticed that she had drawn lines to connect all the dots on the circle she had drawn earlier. The result made him shudder.

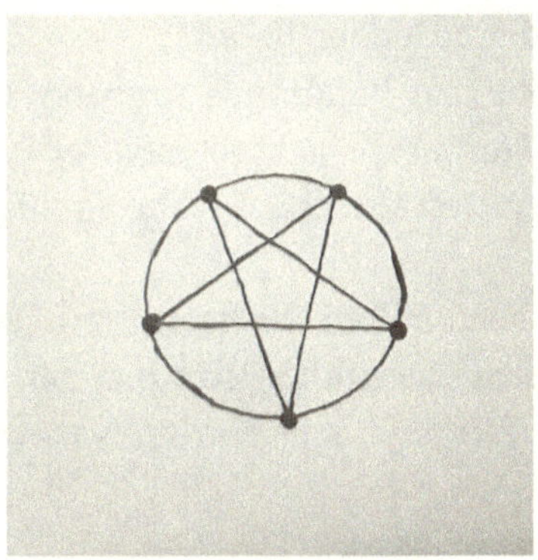

Starting with the bottom-most point, Naomi named each spot while moving clockwise around the circle.

"This first one here is the home of Clarissa/Beverly the mad librarian," she said, tapping the page. "Next is the Little Star Daycare poisonings. After that, we have the Mass Grave of the slaughtered slaves." She offered Graham an apologetic glance when she next mentioned, "Cody's incestuous murder farm," before finally moving on to, "The hanged critters of Beggar's Rock." She then tapped the very center of her pentagram and asked, "What then do you think is here?"

"I don't have to think about it," Graham said. "That's the

Southeastern Archives Repository. It has a reputation for being the place where they house documents which they want kept out of the public's eye yet are too afraid to destroy. There's supposedly a unique copy of Special Field Orders No. 15 in there, as dictated by General Sherman, and written by Lincoln's Secretary of War, Edwin Stanton, with something noteworthy in it which was removed from the copy on display in Sevannah."

"You mean that '40 Acres and a Mule' document?"

"The very one, but it's probably just a rumor."

"Why would it be hidden here?"

"No idea, but that building is probably the second-best secured one in Harborage, next to City Hall."

"Ever been in it?" she asked. "The Archives I mean, not City Hall."

"I haven't," he admitted. "In fact, I've never seen anyone enter or leave that place other than that harpy of a manager they've got, Celeste, and her security. Is that where we have to go to end this?"

"I think so," she sighed.

That answer brought an ever-deepening crease to Graham's brow. "You *think* so?" he asked, letting his exasperation get the better of him. "You mean you don't know?"

She shook her head. "I've been everywhere in this town at least twice, Graham, and when I say everywhere, I mean everywhere, and you wouldn't believe the kinds of secrets that are hidden in the tucked away corners. I've seen some true craziness out there, but the most interesting thing about Harborage was this. A few places were difficult to get into, but only one place was impossible."

"The Southeastern Archives Repository?" he offered.

"The Southeastern Archives Repository," she agreed.

"And that's why you needed the sheriff," he said, understanding dawning on him at last. "That's why you decided that it had to be *me* to help you end this."

Naomi nodded. "Yes."

"What is it you think you'll find in there?"

"I don't know," she said with a shrug. "My mom maybe? She's the smartest person I know, so if we don't find a way to save the world in there, I think at the very least we'll find her, and maybe she'll know what to do. Either way, I know the key to everything is definitely in that building."

"But why is this happening?" he asked. "Why do you have to be the one to end this, and why are you the only one who remembers everything from one loop to the next?"

"I'm not the only one who remembers," she said quietly.

"You aren't?"

"No."

"But who…" he began, before something occurred to him. Only one other person he met during this crazy day seemed to have a specific agenda, and that agenda appeared to involve this person knowing exactly where they needed to go, and exactly what they needed to do without being prompted, prodded, or pushed. This person's actions were fairly tame up to this point, but he had the sinking feeling he might be seeing them again, and that next encounter wouldn't be so tame. "…the clown kid," he said in a near whisper.

"The clown *thing*," Naomi corrected.

"Back at the precinct, you said it was too early, and that the kid wasn't supposed to be there. What did you mean?"

"We've never made it inside the Southeastern Archives Repository," she said, sadly, "because either Clarissa or Cody or something else manages to kill one of us before we get there."

"My cousin has killed me?" he asked somberly.

"A bunch of times," she answered.

"You've actually seen it happen?"

"With my own two eyes."

"How are you still sane?" he asked, in a tone as full of pity as it was of reverence.

"Maybe I'm not," she remarked, giving a laugh that sounded as lifeless and bleak as they both looked. "Anyway, there have only been two times that we both made it past everything this stupid day has thrown at us and reached the road that leads to the Southeastern Archives Repository. Only two times when everything played out perfectly, mean-ing, you came to the precinct; because you don't always show up after Emmett radios you–AND, I convinced you to come with me; because I'm not always able to convince you to come–AND, both of us manage to survive Clarissa; which you know sometimes we don't–AND, both of us survive Cody; which again sometimes we don't–AND, both of us ignore all the other distractions that try to keep us from reaching the Archives. But both of those times, that thing that you think is a kid, and the other thing that you think is a dog, kill us."

"Why do you keep calling them a 'thing'?" he grumbled. "It's just a creepy little kid in a clown costume, and a big dog. That's all."

"Except it isn't though," she insisted. "It's way stronger than it has any right to be, and so is the dog. They pulled both of us out of the car like we were rag dolls, and no matter how hard we fought, we lost."

"How?" he asked, tossing his hands up in surrender and then regretting it as he winced in pain. "Where?"

"The only road leading to the Archives Repository is very narrow," she said, following a heavy sigh. "It's just wide enough for one car, which I'm sure you already know, and it has steep drainage ditches along both shoulders. This idiotic example of modern highway engineering, which was probably meant to discourage any unwanted visitors, cuts through an old forest of thick sturdy trees, that you will undoubtedly hit after sliding down the embankment if you can't manage to stay on the road. All those issues exist year-round, but with it being winter, you can add snow, ice, and an unnaturally early sunset to that list of deterrents. Anywho, both of the times we made it that far, that clown thing stepped into the road just after one of those blind turns, and both times…" Here she paused a moment to stare meaningfully at Graham before continuing. "…you couldn't bring yourself to hit it, so you ran off the road instead, and hit a tree." She took another brief pause, before adding, "We were already pretty beat up from dealing with other things, just like we are now, and we were in no condition to pull ourselves from the wreck, much less put up a fight. The dog ended you with the pointy ends of its teeth, and the clown ended me with the pointy end of a stick."

Graham was too stunned to respond and just sat there contemplating her words. While he was contemplating, and thinking that things surely couldn't get any bleaker, Naomi, having more to say on the subject, spoke, and proved him wrong.

"I've asked you a few relevant questions about this during our other times together," she said, "and I think I know why you can't bring yourself to hit it."

Once again Graham found himself faced with the verbal equivalent of, "Peek not through the keyhole," and hadn't he heard the remainder of that phrase elsewhere? He was quite certain he had no desire to know the answer to the conundrum placed before him now. He was also quite certain he needed to hear it, and if this child…this middle-school student, could continue to brave the horrors that she had been enduring over and over for God only knows how many times, then he had no right to take the cowards way out.

"Why?" he asked.

"Ask yourself this," she offered. "Who do you remember knowing having an albino puppy that used to follow her to the school bus stop every morning, and then meet her at that same bus stop every afternoon? Who had to watch that puppy being run down and left to die in the street by the very same pickup truck used to kidnap her? Who wore their clown outfit to school that Halloween day that she was kidnapped? Who stabbed their kidnapper in the eye with a pencil? And whose head did you later find, also missing an eye?"

"Only the family knew she had been missing an eye," he said in a voice almost too quiet to hear. "We didn't tell anyone else."

"You told me," Naomi said in an equally respectful tone. "I have no idea why little Hailey Finch, or maybe I should say, the thing pretending to be little Hailey Finch, would be trying to stop us from reaching that building, but it definitely is. I didn't bring this up earlier, because I thought that adding murderous ghosts or zombie dogs to everything else I was asking you to accept would be a bit much."

Neither of them spoke for a while, and then into the silence, Graham said, "She blames me."

"No," Naomi said in a matter-of-fact tone. "You had no way of knowing that would happen to her, and you did everything in your power to get her justice. She couldn't possibly blame you."

"She could rightly blame every adult in town," he said. "Because we all knew what a sad sack of hillbilly redneck trailer trash shit Jasper Dalton was. We all knew where he was eventually headed, and we all failed to do anything to change it."

"I don't think you're being fair to yourself," she said. "And I'm not totally convinced that it has anything to do with you, since that thing comes after me, whether you're with me or not. Either way, beating yourself up won't make the decision you're going to have to make any easier."

"Because I'm going to have to decide whether I should kill that child or not," he said, as much to himself as to his companion. "Right?"

"It's not a child, Graham," Naomi consoled. "It's a thing, and it's using your memories of a murdered child to its advantage, and the alternative choice to killing it, is to let *it* kill *you*."

"That's what I'll keep telling myself," he said with a mirthless laugh.

"I never answered your other questions," Naomi reminded him.

"Which other questions?" he asked, sounding thoroughly unconcerned.

"The one about why is this happening?" she said. "And why me?"

"Oh yeah, those."

"Yeah, those, and as far as the 'why me' question is concerned, the best answer I can give is…I don't know."

"I figured as much," he said, putting the car back in drive and pulling away from the curb. "What about the 'why is this happening question?'"

"I only have guesses for that one," she said, sounding thoughtful. "But they're interesting guesses. Wanna hear?"

"Why not," he muttered.

"Great!" she chirped. "I try to think of a new reason each time you ask me, but of course I can't. So far, I just have five halfway decent ones. Please feel free to comment, or to offer one of your own if you like."

Giving her a glance which said he had no intention of doing either, he said, "Will do."

"Okay. So, my first guess is…aliens?"

He grunted to indicate he heard but had nothing to add, so she continued.

"Then I thought maybe…a magic curse of some kind?"

After a few seconds of silence, she went on.

"God has the hiccoughs?" she offered.

He gave a nod of consideration.

"A glitch in the Matrix?"

That one caused him to give a snort of amusement.

"And last, but not least, we're all in Purgatory."

This guess bothered him enough that he gave it a bit of thought before eventually asking, "So, we all died at the same time?"

"I guess," she said with a shrug.

"How?" he asked.

"Nuclear war?" she offered.

After offering the barest hint of a smile, he replied, "Why not."

They drove on in silence for several minutes, until he broke it by asking, "Anything important that I need to know about the Southeastern Archives before we get there?"

"Only that the manager, that woman you mentioned named Celeste, and one of her security guards, an asshole named Dorian, will come to the gate to meet us, and they won't be very welcoming. One of the times I tried to sneak in alone, I got stuck in the razor wire that runs along the top of the gate, and Celeste sent that Dorian guy up to get me. He untangled me from the wire and then literally threw me back outside the gate. That wall he tossed me from has got to be at least thirteen feet high or more, and I broke my leg pretty badly in the fall. I lay there for hours, crying and bleeding until everything finally reset. If the lesson they were trying to teach me was, *don't do it this way again*, I learned it."

"And you think the Southeastern Archives Repository is

another one of those, what did you call them…tainted places?"

"I think it might be the *primary* tainted place," she said, tapping her map. "Ground zero. Ms. Melinoë would probably label it the epicenter of the spiral, which would explain the position of all the other places with pumpkins."

"But why there?" he asked. "All those other places are connected to some past tragedy. What horrible event tainted the archives building?"

Naomi shrugged. "I don't know, but we can probably expect it to be the worst of them all, and considering what I've seen…" She chose to end her sentence with a somber shake of her head.

"Alright then," Graham said, with a grim tone of resignation. "Let's go see what we can find."

9

Graham and Naomi sat in the idling Buick staring at the entrance to the winding driveway which led to their destination. A large and modestly efficient sign proclaimed this to be the Southeastern Archives Repository, 18513 Torpor Ave. Beyond the sign, the road extended into the trees and disappeared around the first bend. The building itself was nowhere in sight, but the nearby sign proclaiming that they were in the right place was easily visible, despite the fading light.

"Doesn't it seem a bit early for the sun to be setting," Graham remarked.

"Yeah," Naomi agreed. "I've often wondered if it was just me, but sometimes time does feel a bit wonky lately."

"Any idea which curve little Hailey is hiding behind?" he asked.

"The road sorta zig zags but there are a few straightaways in-between," she said. "The whole area beyond this point is heavily shaded, and what little sun we're getting can't reach the ground, so the snow and ice are much worse in there than out here. There are six curves total. Three to the left, including that one just inside there, and three to the right. The second left curve is on a hill going up, and the third left is on a hill going down. You used a trick that you said you learned from your father to help get the Buick up that first ice-covered hill. The trick was that you drove with the two wheels of your side of the car just off the road, allowing it to use the gravel and grass to get a bit of traction in the snow."

"That was one of the few things he taught me worth remembering," he remarked.

"Well, it worked," she said, nodding. "Though you didn't use it on the other hill. You said going down on a slope like that was a different story."

"Dad taught me that one too," he said. "And I need to remind myself to stop being amazed when you know things you have no business knowing."

"Good," she said, smiling. "Anywho, Hailey the clown was in a different place both times before, so I don't think we can count on any repeat performances."

"Then we'll take it slow," he said, starting the car forward.

Naomi gave him a worried look. "Are you sure going slow is best?"

"No," he replied. "But it's what we're going to do."

"Okay," Naomi said, leaning back in her seat. "I trust you."

They advanced along the road at a snail's pace, taking particular care when turning into and out of the curves. Graham's anxiety was as high as he could recall it being during the gunfight which scarred their current transportation and based on the number of times she shot glances at the plastic covering the window behind him, Naomi was equally anxious. Graham could not recall the last time he had traversed this road, but he found it to be exactly as his companion had described. It was only wide enough for one car to navigate at a time, with steep inclines on both sides of the road, leading down to small concrete-lined drainage ditches, all almost completely obscured by snow. Just beyond the ditches was a forest which appeared to be as deep as it was dark, populated by numerous wide-trunked trees whose leafless canopy disappeared into the overcast cloud cover high above. Though there was no illumination here beyond the headlights of the Buick, the white of the snow assisted their vision. That same snow, which had frozen over in odd random patches, also added a level of peril which justified their current speed.

"Graham," Naomi said in a hushed tone which seemed quite appropriate for the circumstances. "I need to tell you something before we meet Hailey the clown."

"Is it something you should have told me earlier?" he asked in a tone of accusation, while not taking his eyes off the road.

"No," Naomi insisted. "You knowing this earlier would not have helped us."

"You just said you trusted me," he pointed out, as they rounded the third curve.

"With my life," she assured him. "But I also trust you, to be you."

"I suppose that's fair," he remarked, relieved to find their way unimpeded once they cleared the curve. "Go ahead."

"That plastic on the window back there is a trap for the dog," she said. "Old Mr. Lest Ye Be Vexed."

"How is it a trap?" he asked. "And incidentally, does that hold any meaning for you?"

"You mean the words on the dog's collar?" she inquired.

"Yeah," he replied, nodding.

"Nope," she responded. "And as for the trap, it always uses that way to get into the car. Or at least, it did both the other times. It jumps in and attacks you while we're stuck in the ditch. You shot out my window and told me to climb through the broken glass to get away. I did, or at least I tried to, and that's when Hailey the clown brought the day to a close with its stick. The first time I fought it off long enough to hear the dog win its fight with you, which I never, ever, want to hear again. The second time, I just let it take me."

"Jesus," Graham whispered.

"But this time, things are going to go differently," she assured him. "Because we know how it's going to get in, and I have a plan."

"What is it?" he asked, warily.

"We're going to decide which of them to confront first," she said, "before they have the chance to decide."

"How are we going to do that?" he asked.

"You're going to give me your gun," she began.

"*What?*" he interrupted.

"Just listen, Graham," she insisted. "Okay?"

"...go on," he growled.

"You're going to give me your gun, and you're going to take the sawed-off shotgun hidden in my seat," she said.

He took his eyes off the road for the briefest moment to give his companion an angry glare. "There is no shotgun hidden in your seat," he said in a tone which seemed to say, *I better be right about that*, rather than, *I know I'm right about that*. "There are several secret places all over this car, because it belonged to a drug dealer, but they were all found, and they were all emptied."

"There wasn't a shotgun," she agreed, as she pulled apart a Velcro lined section of her seat revealing the secret compartment housing the weapon. "Until I put one there."

"God dammit, Naomi!" he shouted. "Why the hell didn't you mention this before?"

"Because you would have just taken it and kept it before,"

she pointed out, while she carefully removed the weapon from its hiding place.

"I'm going to take it and keep it now!" he assured her, holding out his hand. "And this is absolutely the worst place and time to be having this conversation!"

"We both need a weapon," she argued, giving the shotgun a shake. "I'm too small to use this one because it has too much of a kick, but I'm pretty sure I can use yours."

"Where did you get that thing?" he demanded, reaching for the gun. "Is it even loaded?"

"The Thompsons, who live two blocks behind the precinct, have an arsenal," she said. "They aren't the only ones who do, but they were the closest. I don't know guns, but I'm pretty sure more than half their stuff is illegal…like their grenade launcher."

"*Their what?*" he said in clear disbelief.

"Yeah," she assured him with a bit of a giggle. "I've brought a premature end to more than one day trying to use that thing, and I've pissed you off more than once trying to convince you to use it."

"Trying to convince me to use a grenade launcher?" he nearly shouted. "On what?"

"Cousin Cody, mostly," she said. "I really hate that fat bastard."

"Watch your mouth," he grumbled.

"Sorry," she said. "Anywho, the Thompson's basement window has a rusted latch, and they're never home."

"But when did you have the chance to put the shotgun in the car?" he asked.

"Before Emmett arrives to work," she said. "There's a gap in your back fence on the east side."

"How did you get the Buick open?" he asked, forgetting about the broken window.

"You keep the keys to all the impounded vehicles in a

locked cabinet in your office," she said. "If I arrive at the precinct when Emmett gets there, crying and claiming to be freezing, it completely interrupts his usual morning process. Once inside, I tell Emmett I need to use the restroom, and I also ask him for something warm to drink. If I time it all perfectly, he leaves his keys on his desk when he goes to put on the coffee that he gives you when you arrive. He makes tea for me. That gives me just enough time to grab his keys, open your cabinet, take what I need, and then put the keys back." After a brief pause, she added, "I don't really need them to get into the car though. It's easy enough to peel back the plastic."

"Then why take them?" he asked.

"It's fun," she said with a shrug. "I've got to do something to keep from losing my mind. Besides, the look on Emmett's face the times he's caught me is priceless."

"Finish telling me your plan," he said, scowling, while bringing the car to a stop. "Because it looks like that's the hill up ahead."

"I think it's fair to assume that it's me the clown and the dog are really after," she said, "judging by the fact that they chase me whether you're with me or not. Having the shotgun should make you an even less desirable target, so if when we see the clown you go out and confront it, the dog should take advantage of me being alone and unguarded. When it jumps through the plastic, I'll be waiting to shoot it." Handing him the shotgun, she added, "And yes, it's loaded."

"Have you ever even used a gun?" he asked, putting the shotgun between his legs with the barrels facing the floor.

"If you mean handguns, I've held exactly two as a matter of fact," she retorted. "One from the Thompsons vast collection which I used to practice, and yours after you dropped it."

After a moment's pause, he said, "I won't ask about any time I might or might not have dropped my gun."

"Good," she remarked.

"But I will ask what you think we should do, if bullets don't work on those two?" he asked.

"If bullets don't work on those two," she considered, "then I guess I'll see you tomorrow." That said, she held out her hand.

"I'll give your idea some thought," he said, ignoring her hand.

"Don't take too long to decide," she warned, looking disappointed. "You never know when our uninvited guests are going to arrive."

Though Graham could vaguely remember being on this road on more than one occasion, he had never bothered to count all the twists and turns. Still, his companion had been right about everything thus far, so it only made sense to accept that she knew what she was talking about. This meant there were only two turns remaining, the next of which was downhill, and a fifty percent chance that little Hailey was around the bend. If she wasn't, then her being beyond the last bend was a certainty, assuming she was here at all.

"It's a coin toss," Naomi said in a solemn tone, apparently reading his mind.

"Don't you dare say heads or tails," Graham mumbled.

"I wasn't," she remarked. "I recognize the inappropriateness, since it's Hailey you're thinking of."

"I actually think there's a better chance she's just around this one," he said, "rather than her being around the last."

Naomi turned to him with a frown of curiosity. "Why?"

"Because it will be much more difficult for me to control

the car going downhill in this snow," he pointed out. "That would work to her advantage."

"Only if you still refuse to run it down," she pointed out. "Then the extra speed would work to *our* advantage, right?"

"All this ice and snow makes any amount of speed dangerous," he reminded her. "And I'm not yet sure I can run over someone's child," he reluctantly admitted.

"I know you aren't," she said in a tone of compassion, which he appreciated, because he knew she would have preferred that he accept her point of view on the matter. He was only able to briefly enjoy that compassion, though, because she destroyed it with the coarsely cheerful tone of her next words. "That's why I brought the shotgun."

They continued to crawl forward at less than 10 miles an hour, edging through the turn so slowly that the trees, which now seemed more ominous and threatening, appeared to creep into and out of their shadowy existence, heralded by the grace of the Buick's two less than perfect cones of amber headlights. Graham let out an audible sigh, when those blessed beams cleared the current thatch of trees and began to shine directly down the snow-covered road ahead. They had made it through the turn, but they still had most of the perilously steep hill to go.

His relief was short lived.

The tiny, billowy shirt had caught his attention because it was adorned with the same huge obsidian puffs Graham remembered seeing before, which were lined up below the frilled collar like fluffy oversized buttons. At the exact base of the hill, where the ice-covered road leveled out, the little broken-doll-faced clown stood unmoving, staring at them with her one good eye. Somewhere during her journey, she had acquired a gnarled stick which was at least a foot taller than she was and was conveniently sharpened to a menacing point on one end. In the hand not holding the stick, the clown held an enormous rock, surely far too large for such a little girl. The scarred dog was nowhere in sight.

Naomi was right again, Graham thought, as he eyed that rock. *Little Hailey there is much stronger than she should be.*

Knowing it was a bad idea yet having no desire to hear that little child's bones crunch beneath the tires of the Buick, Graham attempted to stop the car. Unfortunately, this resulted in a much slower, yet completely uncontrolled descent, and the Buick began to rotate leisurely to the right.

"Graham…" Naomi moaned, while pushing herself back into her seat as if that might put a bit of safe distance between herself and her approaching enemy.

"I know," he said through gritted teeth, as he spun the wheel, attempting to keep the Riviera facing forward. Its weight, which Graham had hoped would help with its stability, worked against it. He dared to give the cumbersome vehicle a bit of gas, while cutting the wheel in the opposite direction of the slide. Gradually, yet ponderously, the spin ceased, and the car began to straighten out. Once they had halved the distance between themselves and the clown, the car was facing forward. Without warning, the windshield shattered into a cobweb of cracks, bringing a scream from Naomi, and a swear from Graham. Little Hailey had obviously thrown her rock. The windshield remained in place but was now impossible to see through. Graham removed his foot from the gas, knowing that hitting even the smallest bare patch of road while he was unable to see might send them careening into the drainage ditch, wherein their fate had previously been decided. Before he could think better of it, Graham drew his revolver and disengaged the safety. "There's a round in the chamber," he barked, handing the weapon to Naomi. "Be careful!"

"I will," she said, taking it.

"With both hands!" he shouted as he grabbed the shotgun. "Point it down until you're ready to shoot!"

"Okay," Naomi agreed, with a tremble of fear in her voice.

After a moment of thought, Graham put the car in park and shut off the engine. The abrupt silence enveloping them was terrifying. With their ears unhampered by the rumble of the motor, the crunch of multiple feet pacing around the slow-moving vehicle could easily be heard, yet the sound's maker was nowhere to be seen. The shrill crash of shattering glass rang out, startling another scream out of Naomi, and making Graham jump in surprise.

The sound was instantly followed by the winking out of one headlight, but Graham was less worried about that than he was thankful that his companion had not accidentally shot herself, or him. In a bout of inspiration, he punched the button turning off the remaining light, hoping that its absence would cause the child to focus on something else.

We're going to need that light, he thought, *if we somehow manage to survive this.*

It seemed that his idea had worked, when no other sounds of breaking glass were heard. Graham squinted through the shattered windshield into the night beyond and thought he could make out the shadowy image of a child holding a stick up as if it were a javelin. Without thinking, he grabbed the child next to him and yanked her toward him moments before the spear shot through the glass and lodged itself in her seat. He was mostly successful, but the tip did manage to slash her shoulder as it passed, causing Naomi to cry out in pain.

Following her scream, two things occurred so suddenly they seemed synchronized. The Hailey-clown leapt onto the hood of the car, quickly grabbing the protruding end of the spear, and the monstrous dog burst through the plastic into the backseat.

Deciding the dog was the more immediate threat, Graham pointed the shotgun toward the backseat and pulled the trigger. At the same time, Naomi pointed the revolver at the thing on the hood and pulled her own trigger in three quick successions. The resounding kapow, and pop pop pop of the two weapons drowned out the shouts of anger and the screams of fright coming from the old man and the girl, as glass rained down from the completely shattered windshield.

The clown, who appeared to have lost the function of one of its arms, still managed to yank the spear from the seat one handed. Shattered collar bone could easily be seen through a hole in the clown's shoulder, yet no blood dripped from the wound. The dog, who somehow managed to survive the pointblank blast of the shotgun, minus a significant portion of its face, lunged forward with its jaws wide, aiming for Naomi's exposed neck. Again, Graham managed to push her out of the way of the deadly attack.

The dog instead sunk its teeth into his arm.

It thrashed back and forth, making it impossible for Graham to chamber the remaining round of the currently useless shotgun. The only thing keeping the beast from ripping off his arm was the tight space it had wedged its head into between the two front seats, and the damage he had done to its jaw with the shotgun. On the hood, the Hailey-clown dropped to its knees, raised the spear above its head, and jabbed down repeatedly, aiming for anything it could reach. Naomi dodged these clumsy thrusts, causing bits of glass to fly from her hair, while the dog's thrashing caused spittle and blood to fly from its mouth. With no care for her own safety, she turned away from her attacker, pushed the muzzle of the gun into the side of the dog's neck, and pulled the trigger until only dry clicks could be heard. After that second volley of pops, the dog slumped silently onto the backseat, its head now only attached to its body by a thin sliver of gristle.

This gave the clown enough time to take careful aim. It did so and brought the spear down with enough force to send its tip tearing into the back of Naomi's parka and the leather seat beyond, pinning her where she was. Graham screamed a breathless, "No!" as he saw the clown bear down with all its weight, driving the tip of the spear through the back of the seat. It wrenched the stick to the side, breaking it in two, just as the sheriff reversed the shotgun and rammed the butt of it into the clown's mask. She, or it, staggered back, giving Graham enough time to turn the weapon, chamber the last round, and shoot the clown in its now partially exposed face. Familiar strawberry-blond hair, barely discernible in the darkness, went flying back as the thing tumbled off the hood.

Seconds later, the car ended its silent slide and came to a halt at the bottom of the hill.

Graham wanted nothing more than to lie down and sleep, or perhaps even lay down and die. It was a morbidly defeatist sort of thought, he knew, but who wanted to continue living in a world where murderous little girls, and murderous monster dogs, who had definitely passed away many years ago, could return to life and kill innocent middle-schoolers who were somehow locked into an unending loop of the same hellish day? Not him, but he couldn't give in to either sleep or death just yet because someone had trusted him, and he needed to know whether he had failed them or not.

With all the care and delicacy he could muster through his pain, Graham brushed aside the bushy hair of the only person who mattered to him at that moment. Just one of her open brown eyes was visible from this angle. Seeing her that way forced images of a child falling backward off the roof of a car into his mind, and he fought back a shudder as well as a few tears which began to blur his vision. He slumped back in his seat to the crunching symphony of broken glass, wondering if there was any way to hold on to the memory of this poor girl, so that he might know her when they met again, for the first time.

———

"Is it over?" came a weak whimper from Graham's right.

"My God!" Graham gasped, feeling both immense pain and immense relief as he sat up and turned. "You're alive!"

"Yeah," Naomi said in a near whisper, her voice thick with emotion. "I think it mostly got my coat," she added, making no attempt to rise, "but it got a good bit of me too."

"The same with the dog," he said, examining the blood-stained fluff sticking out the holes in his sleeve. "Thank God for fleece parkas."

"Graham?" Naomi said with an audible sniff.

"Yes?"

"It hurts."

"I know," he said, swallowing the lump rising in his throat. "I'm sorry."

"Graham?" she sobbed.

"Yes?"

"I don't think I can do this again."

He nodded, sniffed, and examined the back of his hand after wiping away a trail of blood and moisture from his cheeks. "Then let's go make sure you don't have to."

———

A towering steel fence extended across the driveway, securing the gap left by the even higher and more imposing brick wall surrounding the Southeastern Archives Repository. This barrier was all that currently stood between the two odd couples that had recently approached it.

Outside the fence, a few feet from a rusted bullet-riddled Buick with a shattered windshield, stood a short, stout, salt-and-pepper haired older white male, whose grizzled face displayed several small lacerations, and whose once spotless uniform now displayed several holes, as well as both coffee and blood stains. Next to him was a shorter, thinner, frizzy-haired black child, whose once pretty face also displayed several small lacerations, and whose coat and uniform nearly mirrored the condition of the man's beside her. The expressions of this pair spoke of weariness and anger.

Inside the fence, a few feet from a gleaming Mercedes Benz golf cart, stood a tall, slender, salt-and-pepper haired older white female, whose aged beauty and impeccable attire gave her the appearance of a retired runway model, or an early era Hollywood actress. Beside her stood a taller, muscular, bald black male with his arms folded, whose dark suit and menacing countenance would have made a secret service agent proud. The faces of this pair displayed sly, knowing grins, and their attitudes expressed open obstinacy.

"Well Sheriff Graham," the woman chuckled. Her heavy southern drawl made "Graham" a two-syllable word, coming out more like "Gray-yam." "I must say, your appearance leaves me in a bit of a tizzy. I don't know if I should be worried or flattered. You are obviously in desperate need of a doctor. Visiting me couldn't possibly be more important than your health."

"Cut the shit, Celeste," Graham said flatly, skipping the greetings and pleasantries. "Cause I'm in no fucking mood. Open the gate."

"I'm afraid I can't do that Graham," Celeste said, sounding coy.

"Oh?" Graham asked. "What's stopping you?"

"The fact that I don't want to, sugar," she said. Her "sugar" came out closer to "shoo-ga." "And unless you got yourself a warrant, which I know you don't, with both Judge Winley and Mayor Beckett being dear friends of the family and all, the law says I don't have to."

That comment deepened the smile on the face of the man next to Celeste and deepened the scowl on the face of the girl next to Graham.

"Go get yourself looked at Graham," Celeste said with feigned affection. "You've seen better days." She then turned and started toward her golf cart, and her actions were mirrored by her darker companion. Over her shoulder she added, "Auf Wiedersehen," in a teasing tone oddly unblemished by her accent.

Naomi, who had remained silent and still until this point, started forward and opened her mouth to speak but was stopped by Graham's hand gently grasping her shoulder. Graham drew his gun and fired a single round into the fiberglass hood of the golf cart, leaving a large smoking hole with a spider web of cracks radiating from it. Both the occupants leapt away from the vehicle in shock.

"Jesus Christ, Graham!" Celeste shouted as she got to her feet, all her earlier pretentiousness now abandoned. "Have you lost your mind?"

"I'm not gonna ask you twice," Graham growled.

"That's a twenty-thousand-dollar machine!" Celeste spat.

"Oh?" Graham remarked, aiming the gun in her general direction. "And how much is your foot worth?"

"I suppose you aren't aware that the motor's in the back?" Celeste muttered, while brushing bits of dirt and snow from her clothes as she approached the gate.

"Good," Graham said. "We'd prefer not to walk."

After giving Graham a sarcastic smile that faded into a sneer, Celeste punched a code into the keypad set into the wall near the gate and then returned to the cart. The gate gradually retracted into the wall with an ominous silence. Once their advancement was no longer impeded, Graham and Naomi entered, stopping near the ruined hood of the small vehicle.

"Dorian, is it?" Graham asked, eyeing the darker man.

Dorian nodded severely.

"Get yourself on the other side of that there fence, Dorian," Graham said. His gun was lowered, but his tone made it clear this wasn't a request.

Dorian turned his stolid gaze toward Celeste, who gave a silent nod. Naomi passed him as she climbed into the cart. He was beyond the gate when it began to close, where he stood and glared at Naomi. She stuck out her tongue at him in response.

"You're driving," Graham said to Celeste, motioning to the steering wheel with his gun. Celeste slid in behind it without question or comment. Graham then climbed in behind her with a grunt. "Alrighty then," he said, waving his gun in the general direction of the main building. "Let's go."

10

As he stood waiting for Celeste to let them in, it occurred to Graham that they would be walking into this situation completely flat-footed. Neither he nor his little companion knew what to expect, which was probably even more off-putting for Naomi, considering how heavily she had leaned upon her prior knowledge of past events. Neither of them was even sure what they should be searching for, which was particularly troublesome considering the immense size of this facility. Regardless, he was certain this would not be a typical structure designed to secure rare and secretive documents.

He needed only glance at the door itself to confirm this.

On it, a crystalline doorknob was set into a decorative brass plate, below which was an antique-looking keyhole. Unprompted, Celeste pulled a large ancient-looking brass key from a hidden pocket in her blouse. As he watched her use it on the lock, the sheriff ruminated on how ridiculously archaic this was, considering the sleek electronic keypad securing the front gate, but he made no comment.

When she turned the key in the lock, an unusually loud

click sounded, followed by another more distant click from somewhere deeper inside.

The door swung open of its own accord, making the kind of sound one might expect to hear after opening a refrigerator...or violating a tomb.

Naomi was the first to enter.

"There you are, sugar," Celeste said, motioning to the open passage. "Now, if my presence is no longer required..."

"It is," came Naomi's voice from inside. "Don't let her leave, Graham!"

"You heard the little lady," Graham said, motioning to the door. "After you."

"Such a gentleman you are," Celeste crooned, offering a poisonous smile.

She entered after pocketing the key, and Graham followed.

Once inside, he found himself in a startlingly wide and impossibly tall hallway, which extended both ahead and above into the darkness as far as his eyes could see. While he found this somewhat off-putting, particularly regarding the ceiling which shouldn't have been more than twenty feet high based on the view from outside, he soon concluded this was the hallway's least remarkable quality.

Something slightly more bizarre was the hallway's lighting. All nearby illumination was being provided, not by electricity, but by a single tiny candle set high on the wall to his left, which flickered merrily within a smoky beveled sconce. The glass of the sconce was artfully cut in many odd angles, accentuating the capricious nature of the candle's flame, and making Graham feel as if he had stepped into a thirteenth-century English manor. In another setting, this lighting might have been pleasant, but here it only served to bring back memories of a certain basement in Graham's recent past, further souring his mood.

Right beside the ensconced candle stood another oddity: an unusual door. In contrast to the surrounding walls, which were painted the typical eggshell white of any number of building interiors, this door was bright pink. On it was a Dr. Seuss-like cartoonish drawing of a large white stork in mid-flight, laboring to carry an even larger white bundle in its beak. Written on the bundle were the words, "It's a Girl." This was indeed peculiar for a door in a supposed archives repository, but its peculiarity didn't end there. The door was at least twice as tall and twice as wide as the door they had just come through, and its bulbous knob was so large Graham believed he would have to grab it with both hands to turn it, and even then, he was sure opening it would still be a struggle. What kind of person would such a door be made for, he wondered, before quickly deciding he didn't want to know, considering how his day had gone thus far.

Squinting down the dimly lit hall, he saw that there was another candle-filled sconce and another enormous door set on the opposite side of the hall roughly thirty feet from where he stood. This next door and candle-sconce pair appeared to be identical to the first in nearly every way, except the door did not display the same cartoonish stork decoration. Even farther down the hall, barely visible in the fickle light, was yet another door and candle-sconce pair on the same side of the hall as the first. Noting them brought his attention to the hallway's next oddity: the obscure paintings.

These curious works of art covered most of the wall space where doors and candles didn't exist. They were of various shapes and sizes and housed in frames of equally varying imagination and creativity. Some of the frames were made of nothing more elaborate than dark wood polished to a perfectly reflective shine, while others were made of interwoven rainbow hued peacock feathers, and still others were made of a thatch of thorny vines and blood-red roses. The subjects of the paintings appeared to be people, though it was difficult to tell because all were blurred beyond precise recognition, as if they had been created by the hands of a precocious toddler who only possessed a rudimentary knowledge of how people are supposed to look. Also, and Graham had to admit to himself that he wasn't quite sure of this, the images appeared to shift slightly as if the people depicted within were restless. He never saw them move or change because they remained still while he stared directly at them, but if he glanced back after turning away, something about them seemed different. He found that he had to exert genuine effort to keep his eyes from darting from one portrait to the next in an attempt to catch them changing, making him feel like he was playing a twisted game of Red Light-Green Light with what should have been inanimate objects.

Hoping to create a sense of stability, Graham allowed the investigator within him to take over, noting patterns wherever they were to be found. From that perspective, the general arrangement of the interior seemed to be: one lit candle in a decorative glass setting hung on alternating sides of the hall every thirty feet or so, set beside a door meant for a smallish giant, with oddly shaped and indistinguishable paintings covering all the wall space in-between, which occasionally decided to move when you didn't give them enough attention.

This arrangement was, of course, more than peculiar for a place of business, and after glancing at his feet, Graham wasn't surprised to find the floor equally strange, if "floor" was the correct word to use. Rather than it being carpeted, most of the area beneath his feet consisted of a multihued cobblestone path, which meandered snakelike down the hallway, leading from one oversized door to the next. The rest of the floor not covered by the cobbled walkway was blanketed by what appeared to be an emerald green lawn. The stones of the path were as neatly arranged and as orderly as jigsaw puzzle pieces, while the grass grew in haphazard clumps and random tufts where an occasional flower sprouted with no apparent need for sunlight.

Adding yet another touch of strangeness, the chirp of crickets could be heard, and the twinkle of firefly lights could be seen from within the tufts, but no other evidence of either insect was present. This presentation gave Graham the overall feeling of being in the Mad Hatter's idea of an indoor botanical garden, rather than a government sanctioned development.

With a bit of trepidation on Graham and Naomi's part, and sullen reluctance on Celeste's, the group cautiously made their way down the hall. Naomi led, dutifully following the cobbled path, yet giving little scrutiny to the doors she passed, which continued to appear on alternating sides of the hall, maintaining their unusual size and shape.

"What's the point of all this?" Graham asked, roughly nudging Celeste.

"The point of all what?" Celeste said without turning.

"I think you know what I mean," Graham said. "This doesn't look like any archives facility I've ever seen."

"How about you ask your little friend there?" Celeste responded sourly.

"You're the one who works here!" Graham growled, giving her a bit of a shake. "So, I'm asking *you.*"

"Look!" Naomi shouted before sprinting off down the hall.

"Don't get too far ahead!" Graham bellowed as he struggled to keep up.

He passed many gloomy hallways leading off to the right and left, some of which presented equally gloomy staircases leading up or down, and though Naomi had disappeared into the shadows, he somehow instinctually knew not to detour from the main path. He finally caught up to his companion, finding her standing beside a door lying on the ground. It looked as if it had been torn from its frame, leaving its nearby doorway gaping wide. The candle had also been torn off the wall and lay in the grass beside the door, unlit. The room, which had once been secured by the colossal door was completely dark and offered no clue as to what might lie beyond its flat arch. Naomi did not seem to be concerned about the contents of the room and just stood staring down at a plate set in the middle of the door. Graham glanced down at the plate, read the name written on it, and then asked the nearby child the most obvious question that came to mind.

"You wouldn't happen to know anybody named Malik, would you?"

"My father's name is Malik," Naomi said, still staring down at the plate. "But I don't really know him. I've only met him once, briefly, during a trip Mom and I took to Africa. Mom said she met him at Holme University where they both attended. He's supposedly the son of a foreign dignitary or something, and apparently his well-to-do family didn't approve of her. He seemed like a nice enough guy and all, but he didn't give me the impression he was in any way interested in being a parent." With a glance toward the darkened room, she added, "He does send money sometimes and an occasional birthday card. I seriously doubt this has anything to do with him though."

Graham turned his questioning gaze to Celeste, who shrugged in response. He opened his mouth to ask whether she knew anything at all about the place she came to work in every day, when again Naomi dashed off down the hallway shouting, "Look!" With a pained grumble he followed, keeping the Southeastern Archives Repository manager closely in tow. He passed a few more candle-sconce/large pink door pairs and paintings, as well as one staircase leading down into the shadows, before catching up to his companion. She was standing at the apparent end of the hall, staring at two doors which barred any further advancement. These doors were just as pink as the others, and they each shared their space with the usual candle, but they were much smaller than the previous doors. They were, in fact, nearly normal-sized, and possessed nearly normal-sized knobs. Several words were written directly onto both doors in either black ink or black paint. The words on the door to the left were smeared into unintelligibility by what seemed to be a purposeful hand, while those on the right were quite neat and clear. Graham followed the readable words in his mind as he heard Naomi say them aloud, noting that she sounded just as baffled by them as he.

"'She will be attending Heaton,'" she read. "'I may have to pull a few strings, but I'll get her into that pre-k one way or another.'" Just below this sentence was a name, which she also read aloud, sounding even more confused. "'Ellanor.'" Its presence gave the impression that the sentence above was a quote.

Graham was on the verge of asking another question, which he was certain Naomi had no answer for, when a startlingly loud bang came echoing down the hall from the direction from which they had come. The noise caused both he and Naomi to jump in surprise and turn to stare down the darkened hall behind them, while Celeste, who appeared unconcerned, yawned. The bang was quickly followed by louder echoing bangs, which again caused the startled pair to jump.

"What the hell is that?" Graham demanded, giving Celeste a shake.

"I think you'd have to call that *unfinished business*, sugar," she replied, smiling.

"Your man Dorian?" he asked, putting his hand on the butt of his gun.

"Oh, no dear," she said in a tone of feigned sympathy. "I'm pretty sure Dorian is out of the picture."

"Then who–" The echoing sounds of what was surely splintering wood interrupted him.

"That would be the front door," Celeste said in a cheerful tone. "Dorian isn't capable of something like that." Turning her smile to the sheriff, she asked, "You wouldn't happen to know anyone who would be, would you sugar?"

Again, Graham opened his mouth to respond, and again he was interrupted, this time by a series of loud and wet-sounding barks echoing down the hall. "Shit!" he swore.

"Indeed," Celeste agreed, somewhat jovially.

"I think we better go, Graham," Naomi said, sounding as unnerved as he felt.

She reached for one of the doorknobs without turning, and her hand found the one on the left. Graham heard her attempt to open it. He also heard the knob catch before opening, making it clear that it was locked. Turning toward the door, he saw her give it a few more panicked shakes before giving up. She grasped the other knob and then hesitated. Giving him a look which was the visual equivalent of *Cross your fingers*, she turned.

There was no resistance, and the door easily swung open to reveal another hallway beyond. This hall was very different from the previous one, but that was their least concern. The teenager rushed through the arch, quickly followed by the old man, who dragged the old woman in his wake. The group took a moment to gaze down the shadowy hall from which they had come. There was neither movement nor sound in that direction now, but Graham would have sworn that he felt something, which only if forced to, he would grudgingly have defined as a malevolent presence approaching. Hoping to avoid seeing the physical representation of what his mind insisted could not possibly be the dead child and dead dog they left on the snow-covered road, he grabbed the door and slammed it shut. After noting what appeared to be a keyhole set into the frame of this side of the door, he turned to Celeste.

"The key!" he demanded.

Without a word, the old woman reached into her blouse and produced the old-fashioned key which she had used earlier on the front door. The sheriff snatched it from her and shoved it into the lock. It gave an audibly satisfying click as he turned it, and again, only if forced to, he would have grudgingly admitted that it appeared to lessen the feeling of malevolence and approaching doom.

"I'll hold on to this," he grumbled, slipping the key into his pocket.

"Suit yourself, sugar," Celeste said with a shrug.

In near unison, the trio turned to assess the new environment, and what was presented to them was no less surprising, and no less confusing than the area they had just vacated. As before, the hallway bore uncarpeted ground, but rather than a grass/cobblestone arrangement, it now offered a combination of grass and what appeared to be an unremarkable-looking sidewalk. The walls were more colorful here, with the one on the left side being sky blue, and the one on the right being lemon yellow. The doors here were only slightly larger than ordinary, and seemed to have the same distance between them, alternating sides just as before, but they were a shade of purple which Graham guessed would have probably been referred to as lilac, or something equally fancy. This hall was also lit by ensconced candles, which were just as dim as before, but its kaleidoscope like motif made everything seem brighter and more jovial. The paintings here were just as indistinguishable as the previous ones and their frames just as varied, and they also appeared to move and shift in the same way as the others had when they weren't being scrutinized…maybe. It made Graham feel as though he had returned to grade school for some reason, and the nostalgia of it briefly took his mind off the possible horror which might or might not be following.

Again, Naomi took the lead, following the sidewalk down the hall, avoiding the grass and ignoring the doors. She set a fast pace, which Graham was both thankful for, due to their unknown pursuer, and begrudging of, due to his many muttering injuries. He was giving his wounds a quick assessment when Naomi came to a halt beside a door which was slightly ajar. She caught his full attention when her hands rose to cover her open mouth.

"Oh my God," the child whispered through her fingers. "I forgot about that shampoo she used to use! It made him smell like a baby."

A thick swirling blue-gray mist caught Graham's eye as it churned within the unlit room beyond the door. It evaporated as soon as it drifted into the hallway, leaving behind the unmistakable fragrance of talcum powder. Purposefully avoiding touching the door, Graham moved to peer around it to get a look at the front. On it, at the height one would expect to see a motel room number, was a brass plate engraved with the name, "Max".

"Max?" he asked, turning to Naomi.

"He was Gran's Pomeranian," she said with a nostalgic grin. "Don't you hear the barking?"

Graham reluctantly leaned a little closer to the swirling mist and was surprised to find that he could indeed hear the distant sounds of barking. It was actually closer to a series of high-pitched yaps which were a heartwarmingly welcome sound, particularly after hearing the hideous noises being made by the horrors hunting them. "You don't think he's in there, do you?" he asked.

"No," Naomi said, shaking her head. "I think it's a trick of some kind, maybe to trap us in the room or slow us down." Smirking, she added, "Gran treated that dog as if it was her other grandchild. Sometimes I even thought she loved it mo–" Her words were interrupted by another disturbingly familiar bang which echoed down the hall. After a worried glance behind them, Naomi said, "We should go," and then trotted off. Graham quickly followed, dragging Celeste along by her arm.

"Just what the hell is all this?" Graham murmured, giving Celeste a brisk shake, which caused her to miss a step and nearly stumble.

"I told you to ask your little protégé," she returned angrily. "She would know better than I."

"You're the manager of this damned facility!" he barked.

"You sure about that?" the old woman asked.

"If you're asking whether I'm sure you run the place–" he began.

"I'm not," she interjected. "I'm asking if you're sure it's a facility."

The two glared at one another, his reddened face displaying both irritation and confusion, and her pale face displaying cynicism and apathy. Graham was on the verge of demanding further explanation when his attention was drawn by a call from Naomi up ahead.

"Come on Graham!" the girl shouted, waving at them from around a corner she had taken.

Graham was grateful she had waited because the area was an intersection. A sign with multicolored lettering dangled from a pair of chains which stretched up into the shadows of the apparently nonexistent ceiling. The sign read: Geisel

Manor. The sheriff's knowledge of Harborage County landmarks wasn't nearly as thorough as he wished it to be, but he was certain Geisel Manor was the name given to the Pre-K and Kindergarten buildings of Heaton Academy, in honor of Theodore Geisel, who was more commonly known as Dr. Seuss.

Graham turned this corner, still dragging an increasingly irritated Celeste, as the bangs behind them got louder. Further ahead, he saw Naomi turn another corner, and when he reached this intersection, the sign hanging from the shadowy air above read: Curie House. Graham had no idea what a Curie House was, but he supposed it might be the name given to yet another building at Heaton Academy, likely the next few grades up from kindergarten. Several candles, doors, paintings, and dark hallways later, Naomi turned at yet another intersection. Reaching the hanging sign here which read Tubman House, Graham found his concern growing over whether the child knew where she was going, because given the circumstances, he had no idea how she possibly could.

Immediately after turning the corner, the group came to another end, where again they faced two doors barring any further advancement. The door on the left matched the color of the left wall, which was sky blue, and the door on the right matched the lemon-yellow hue of the right wall. Each door shared its space with an ensconced candle, which wasn't a surprise, but these doors were the exact size and shape one would expect a door to be, which was. Just as before, several words were written directly onto the doors, and just as before, the words on the door to the left were smeared into unintelligibility, while those on the right were clear and legible. Once again, Graham followed the words in his mind as he heard Naomi say them aloud, and once again, she sounded confused.

"'There's no way in hell I'm going to uproot her and move to Africa just to be a part of your harem…'"

Just as before, there was a name below the words whose presence made them feel like a quote.

"Kenisha…?" Naomi read, sounding bewildered.

"Does that mean anything to you?" Graham asked.

"I might be wrong," Naomi ventured, "but I think I remember overhearing my mom saying these exact words to my father one night when he called."

"You think that's a quote from your mother?" Graham inquired doubtfully.

"I think so…," Naomi replied, obviously preoccupied with her thoughts. "Mom's name is Kenisha. And Ellanor is Gran's name, so maybe that other quote was supposed to be Gran's."

Remembering that they had at least two very disturbing reasons not to tarry and recalling how things turned out with the previous door, Graham said, "Try to open the one on the left."

Naomi tried and found it locked. After giving him a brief knowing glance, she tried the other door. It opened easily. Without hesitation, she stepped through. Celeste came next, having been shoved roughly through by the man who followed her. Graham then shut the door, noted the keyhole, removed the key from his pocket, and slid it into the lock.

"Not sure if I ever knew a Kenisha," he said, turning the key in the lock to secure the door. "But I did know an Ellanor once. She–"

There was a loud boom as something hit the other side of the door with enough force to rattle it in its frame. Graham and Naomi jumped in fear and alarm. Celeste merely smiled. Another boom followed, knocking the key from the lock.

"Time to go," Graham said, retrieving the key and returning it to his pocket.

Nodding in agreement, Naomi turned and led the way.

The hall was quite a bit brighter and narrower now, and Graham was surprised to find that the doors were now all the typical size. Being more focused on getting some distance between the group and the door behind them, he didn't notice any other difference in the doors until he saw Naomi giving them a little more attention than she had the previous ones. A glance at the next one he passed explained why. These new doors, which still bore a lilac hue, now had small square windows in them set just beside the knob. As he continued down the hall, the brighter illumination helped him notice something else he hadn't before, causing him to slow in his progress and stare despite all other concerns.

This new revelation disturbed him in a way that no other oddity had this bizarre day, which was quite an accomplishment, considering, and it made him wonder whether they had made a mistake coming to this place.

What he saw was that the occupant of every single painting visible from where he stood was turned to face Naomi as she made her way down the hall. The paintings were quite a bit darker and more shadowy, but they were not as blurry and undefined as before. He still found it impossible to discern exactly who the people in the paintings were meant to be. Yet there was no doubt in his mind that all of them were following the young girl's progress. They still refused to change while he was staring at them, but each time his eyes drifted away from and then returned to a painting, the occupant was slightly different. *And it's not just their eyes either,* he thought as he saw Naomi turn a corner ahead. *Their whole body is turned to face the exact spot where she was, but she doesn't seem to notice it.* He returned to a faster pace when a distant bang reminded him that they were being pursued. As he approached the corner, he wondered whether it would be a good idea to bring the painting issue to Naomi's attention.

When he turned the corner, what he saw drove that thought from his mind and caused him to stop abruptly.

There were far fewer paintings in this new hall, due to them being much larger than any of the previous ones. Their shadowy visage hadn't changed and neither had their slight blur, but the larger-than-life occupants within these frames were all turned to stare angrily down at him. He supposed the paintings could have been arranged to look as though they were staring at the place someone would have to stand when they turned that corner, but he doubted it, because none of them appeared to be staring at the woman beside him. *It's like they knew I was considering telling the girl about them,* he thought, *and it pissed them off.*

Another loud bang from behind got him moving again, though doing so with the weight of those stares pressing down on him made progress nearly unbearable. He soon caught up with the girl he had been following, but only because she had stopped in front of a burgundy-hued door with a single stripe of azure running down the center. Graham never would have used such fancified words to describe what in his mind was simply dark red and dark blue before meeting the girl standing nearby, but he now did because he knew them to be the correct terms, seeing as how they matched the colors in her Heaton uniform exactly. He turned and peered into the window of the nearby door, certain he was about to see something just as peculiar as all the other peculiar somethings he had seen thus far.

He wasn't disappointed.

There, apparently growing in the center of the room, its position accented by dim yet distinct spotlights, stood an exquisitely beautiful tree. The tree appeared to be an impossible interbreeding of a gnarled and ancient weeping willow and an extremely vivid species of wisteria, and though he couldn't put his finger on it, Graham was sure he had seen that tree somewhere before.

"That," Naomi said, pointing at the tree beyond the window, "is The Violet Lady. She's in The Alumni Grove at Heaton, which separates the boys' residences from the girls'." Turning to stare directly at Celeste, she added, "This is the exact view I have of her from my dorm room window in Tubman House."

Celeste, who appeared to be completely uninterested in anything Naomi had to say, was studying the nails on her hand from various angles and made no comment.

"Why does everything in this place seem to have something to do with me?" Naomi demanded.

"I think you already know the answer to that question, dear," Celeste responded in open contempt.

"If I did, I wouldn't have asked you," Naomi retorted with equal disdain. "In fact, I would prefer not to have to look at you, much less speak to you."

"That can be easily remedied," Celeste pointed out while gesturing to the wrist Graham continued to hold. "Just call off your bodyguard and I'll be on my way."

"For fucks sake, Celeste," Graham barked, giving her a shake. "Just answer the girl!"

The old woman turned her icy gaze to the old man, and opened her mouth to speak, when a crash which rivaled the first resounded from the hall where they had come. Just as before, the crash was quickly followed by a series of loud and wet sounding barks.

"You know, sugar, I'm not quite sure I remember the answer," Celeste said, giving Graham a coquettish smile. "Why don't you give me a minute or two to collect my thoughts?"

Turning away in anger, Naomi resumed her progress

down the hall, announcing over her shoulder, "We're ignoring every door that isn't in our way here on out."

Graham spared a moment to shake his head at Celeste in disgust and was about to step away when a bit of motion beyond the window caught his eye. Peering through for the second time, he noticed a recent addition to the scene. Sitting beside the tree, staring meaningfully in Graham's direction, was an enormous wolf with silver-white fur and moon-yellow eyes. For some inexplicable reason, the beast was clad in an oversized Heaton Academy uniform identical to the one that Naomi wore beneath her Parka, including the skirt (which all fit it surprisingly well) but minus the shoes. The outfit should have made it comically ridiculous but instead made it ominously surreal. It being the only other living thing any of them had seen since they entered the facility, he was briefly tempted to call Naomi back to get a look at it as well, but the echo of a gurgling growl from behind made him think better of it. He left the door feeling a slight tinge of regret, feeling he had been forced to abandon a definite middle piece to his puzzle, as he proceeded after his ward with the manager in tow.

Ahead he saw Naomi turn another corner, and he also saw that the paintings had returned their attention to her, which she still did not seem to have caught on to. When he reached this corner and turned it, he found his first somewhat pleasant surprise since they had entered this place. This new hall was exactly the width and height one would expect in a place of business, with a clearly visible ceiling from which squares of basic fluorescent lighting were attached. The entire floor was carpeted in an amiably neutral earth tone. The walls had returned to the eggshell white which he had seen near the main entrance, and were, mercifully, completely void of doors and paintings. Naomi stood nearby, staring down this new and apparently normal hallway with a look of trepidation.

"This makes me feel even more nervous than the other halls did," Naomi said in hushed tones. "Like the proverbial calm before a storm."

Graham thought so as well but kept it to himself. "We should go," he reminded her.

"Right," Naomi agreed and headed off again, setting a fast pace.

After a few minutes of walking, Graham realized what this hallway's oddity was. Each of the squares of fluorescent light attached to the ceiling above appeared to be spaced roughly three feet apart, and the sheriff was relieved to find that they kept the immediate area near the small group lit quite well. Unfortunately, the same could not be said for the lighting in the distant hallway both ahead and behind. The reason for this became apparent as soon as one of the lights ahead of them blinked into existence as they advanced, and one of the squares behind them winked out.

Now that he was paying closer attention, Graham realized that there were never more than three lights illuminated above them in either direction. This unfortunate truth ensured that they would be both pursued by and in pursuit of whatever mysteries the shadows concealed. He asked Naomi to pause for a moment to confirm this and discovered something much worse. As they stood there waiting, one square behind them winked out, and one ahead blinked on. Though the group had ceased their advancement, the lights had not, and if they remained where they were, they would soon be plunged into complete darkness.

"Shit," Graham swore, as he and the others got moving again.

"I guess we aren't the ones setting the pace," Naomi said.

After a glance at his many wounds, she asked, "Is it moving too fast for you?"

"I'll manage," he assured her, taking a weary look over his shoulder. "Don't worry about me."

They walked for several uneventful minutes, struggling to keep up with the shifting illuminated squares above, until the furthest light ahead shined on another set of doors at the apparent end of the hall. The lights continued to wink out as they approached the doors, until only three squares remained, keeping this small section of the hallway adequately lit. Graham noted that there were many similarities between this set of doors and the ones they had passed through earlier, but there were also a few differences. There were no candle-filled sconces in sight this time, which he thought was understandable considering the brightness of the overhead lights. As before, the door on the left was painted the same off-white hue as the nearby wall, and it displayed another set of words which were again smeared into unintelligibility, yet neither the color of, nor the contents on the door on the right could be seen, because the door wasn't there. It appeared to have been removed from its hinges, which were still attached to the frame, though whether this had been done with tools or by violence, Graham was unsure.

The three of them stood before this open passage and peered warily into the gloom beyond. An ill wind blew past them from behind, carrying with it a scent which was not quite a reek but was unquestionably unpleasant.

Other than their breathing, which was slightly labored on the part of the older man and woman, there were no sounds. Within the next room, quite a distance from where they stood, Graham could see the other door lying on the ground. The side with the words written on it were faced up, but the surrounding shadows prevented him from reading them.

Beyond the door on the ground, he thought he could just make out the dimmest glimmer of light illuminating what appeared to be a dead end. He prayed that was not the case, because if it was, then it would be here that they would have to make their final stand against…

"Graham," Naomi said in a croaked whisper, which dripped with all the fear she had been suppressing until now.

He knew what he would see before he turned to follow Naomi's gaze.

He had absolutely no desire to see that child… no, that thing, that was pursuing them again, but he was the sheriff. He was the duly appointed representative of authority here, and it was his job, as well as his willingly adopted responsibility, to protect the girl next to him. There was no way to accomplish that goal without facing what he was protecting her from, so with the greatest reluctance he had ever felt, Graham turned.

He was not always proud of the choices he had made in life. Who was? Still, when Graham got to heaven, if he somehow managed to earn such a reward, he seriously planned to ask God what the exact sin was that he had committed to deserve to have to confront this horrid travesty which had once been someone's beautiful baby girl. She, or it, stood in the shadowy area just beyond the last square of light, but Graham was certain she wouldn't remain there for long. Regardless, the shadows did little to hide the shambling ruin that was Hailey Finch.

The frilled neck ruffle and surrounding billowy blouse which had been riddled with holes from the earlier confrontation, hung limply from the tiny clown's frame, making the damage Naomi had done with the handgun (a broken and clearly exposed collarbone) quite evident. This appeared to make the use of that arm difficult, judging by the way it hung limply at Hailey's side. In its other hand, it held the sharpened stick, which it used as an oversized walking staff. The shotgun blast from Graham, which should have ended the thing's existence, had driven the broken shards of the mask the thing had been wearing into the newly created cavity in the side of its head. Bits of the shattered mask were quite indistinguishable from bits of brain and skull in that gaping hole, which was somehow void of blood. Half of its face was spared most of the destruction, allowing it to retain part of its now demonic looking porcelain doll grin, behind which the remanence of tiny broken teeth could be seen. For some inexplicable reason, the thing had decided to retrieve its pointy hat before continuing its hunt, which now tilted slightly to one side due to the missing parts of its head. Beneath that less than jovial crown, a few errant strands of strawberry-blond hair could be seen, as well as a single glaring blue eye.

Graham saw an accusation in that single blue eye. It was an accusation which if given voice, seemed to say, *if you had protected me back then the way you are protecting her now, I wouldn't be here.* Knowing that such thoughts were just a sadistic personification of his guilty conscience didn't stop him from wanting to explain his failure. It didn't stop him from wanting to apologize. Graham was about to utter the words to that explanation, or to that apology, when Hailey took a single step forward, drawing a horrified gasp from the girl next to him.

He wished she hadn't stepped forward.

He wished this was all just a bad dream he could force himself to wake from, but somehow it wasn't. Somehow, and for some inexplicable reason, in the hand he had believed to be useless, the shattered faced clown child held the severed head of her dog. It dangled at her side, with her tiny fingers clutching one of its ragged ears, and worse, the thing still continued to snarl and bark.

Not possible, Graham reasoned, as his mind struggled to make sense of what he was seeing. He drew his gun more out of instinct than any conscious thought and backed the group through the open doorway as the broken clown continued its pursuit. The lights above it winked out with each step, keeping the Hailey-clown partially shrouded in shadows, and making it clear that sight was about to become a luxury they could not afford. Once they were beyond the door, Graham reached to shut it, and his hand met with empty air. With a sinking in his gut reminiscent of the time he made the mistake of glancing down from the top floor of the Empire State Building, he remembered the door wasn't there. He continued to push the group further into the dark room with grim reluctance, while motioning for them to back up. A glance behind told him that the child whose life he was determined to protect, and the woman whose life he would begrudgingly protect, were several steps away. Good, he thought, as he raised his shaking gun and pointed it at the child whose travesty of a life he was determined to end.

His vision of the broken clown as it advanced was blurred by tears, and Graham brought up his other hand to steady both his gun and his resolve. He took a deep breath, then slowly let it out in preparation for the shot, as the once-Hailey stopped in the open doorway. The last thing Graham saw before the light winked out and left them in near darkness, was the clown-thing's tiny body twist and spin where it stood, as it heaved the still snarling head of the monster dog right at him.

It took all his concentration to fight the impulse to raise an arm in self-defense. Doing so would mean sacrificing the mental lock he had on the last known location of the demented child. He felt the beast's teeth split the flesh of his cheek as it passed, causing him to peel off a single shot in surprise. The muzzle flash illuminated the room for a single heartbeat, and in that moment Graham saw the swiftly approaching end of his life.

The Hailey-thing had halved the distance between them in a silent sprint, holding the spear before it as if it were a jousting lance. Graham shot twice more before the tiny thing hit him with what felt like the force of a miniature bull. It drove him to the floor, knocking his breath from him. He shot four times more and was certain that at least two of them found their mark. Each flash offered him a horrid glimpse of the clown taking aim with its stick as it moved to straddle the old man, but its sights weren't set on him. Its focus was trained on a smaller target which had moved in to engage the thing.

"Naomi no!" Graham shouted, as the thing thrusted its spear into the darkness. "Get back!"

There was a muffled thud, followed by a scream of anguish. Graham thrust the muzzle of his gun into the thing's neck and pulled the trigger twice more. For the briefest moment, there was an ominous silence, and all was still. Without warning, the stick arced from the darkness and knocked the gun from his hand. With his eyes now partially adjusted to the gloom, Graham could just barely make out the shadowy image of the horrid jester as it raised the stick above its now lolling head, its murderous intent obvious. He raised his hands to shield his face as the first thrust pierced through his parka and ripped open the skin above his collarbone. The thing wrenched the spear violently to one side before raising it again, and it was only luck which allowed Graham to keep the spear from slicing open his jugular as it passed. The thing paused, as if to take better aim this time, and the old man knew it was preparing to put the next thrust through his heart.

A hand reached out and grabbed the spear, twisting with surprising force. A feral sounding scream that could only be

Naomi's pierced the silence, as a shadow which was darker than the surrounding darkness moved to position itself behind the clown. Using its own weapon against it, Naomi forced the stick under the thing's chin, holding it in place with her hands on either side of its head. She screamed as she pulled the stick against the clown's neck with all the strength her little body could muster.

But it wasn't enough. Though it only had a single hand to defend itself, that hand was more than capable. The once-Hailey grasped the stick, now quivering with Naomi's struggle, and pulled. The stick began to move away from its neck. Graham grasped the thing's hand with both of his own. In a slow and horrid dance which felt as if it lasted hours, the old man pried the thing's grasping fingers from the stick.

With renewed screams of effort, Naomi leaned back and pulled. There was a loud ripping crunch, and a wet sounding crack, which Graham was sure had been the snapping of the stick, until he saw Naomi fall backward, and he felt Hailey's hand go limp.

A long and ominous silence followed, eventually broken by the muffled sobs of a young girl, and the sound of a tiny headless body slumping to the floor. Graham pushed the corpse away and got to his feet as quickly as his numerous injuries would allow, intent on preventing his young companion from seeing exactly what she had done.

"Close your eyes and let me have this," he said to the girl as he gently grasped the stick. The flood of emotions he was feeling made his words nearly unintelligible, but Naomi must have understood because she opened her trembling hands and released the weapon. He took it and tossed it away, not caring where it went, hearing it clatter off to one side. He then reached down to his companion, wishing that he could lift her into his arms, yet knowing that all the insane stresses of this nightmarish day would only allow him to help her stand.

As the still sobbing child got unsteadily to her feet, he noted the nearby melon-shaped shadow which denoted the location of a tiny, decapitated head. Recalling that the dog's disembodied parts had somehow managed to hold on to some profane parody of life, he fought the urge to kick the malformed melon into the far corner. He was about to lead a sniffling Naomi away from what remained of Hailey Finch, when a single dim bulb winked back into existence just beyond the open doorway. Taking this as a sign that another dark chapter of their journey had been concluded, Graham turned to leave but then turned back and examined the door on the ground. Though weak, the illumination made the words easily legible. They read:

She's never had a birthday party before, Mom. I really want to get her something nice for this first one.

As with the others, there was a name beneath this presumed quote. This time the name read: Naomi.

Clueless of the implications that this new bit of information offered, Graham committed it to memory as best he could and then ushered his ward away from the body of the headless clown, deeper into the belly of this mad facility.

A few steps brought them to where the hallway did indeed end in a "T" junction. The light Graham noted earlier issued from a single naked bulb hanging from the ceiling, again oddly reminiscent of a certain librarian's torture basement. Standing beneath the bulb in a silent statement of open obstinance was Celeste. Behind her, three red doors stood side by side against the far wall of the junction. A palpable air of foreboding drifted from those doors, as if unease had an actual stench, giving the moment a dreadful sense of finality. Was the answer to the mystery of the town's many horrors beyond those doors, Graham wondered, and did those horrors all somehow connect to Naomi? If so, he wasn't sure he was ready to know. Naomi, however, didn't share his reluctance. After wiping the tears from her cheeks, she made her way to the end of the hall.

"Never occurred to you to help I suppose," he growled as he passed Celeste to join the child.

"That was *your* unfinished business, sugar, not mine," she returned, displaying not an ounce of shame.

Successfully suppressing a retort which would have undoubtedly involved many choice bits of profanity, Graham considered the new information he had just acquired, and how it might connect to the information he had acquired earlier. *Three quotes, made on three different occasions, by three members of the same family,* he pondered. *Only, this third one doesn't quite fit.* Laboring under the assumption that the first two were indeed made by Naomi's grandmother and mother respectively, he believed those first two statements were the kind one might call *life altering,* while that last just seemed to be some random trivial event. Life altering or not, why were they being displayed so prominently on the doors of this peculiar facility, who had put them there, and what on earth could they possibly have to do with the theorized "God's hiccough" repeating day?

The best way to begin to unravel those knots, he thought, would be to ask his little companion if she had indeed made that statement, and if she had, what had she meant by it. If that shed no light on the mystery, he decided he might have to be a little more persuasive with their unwilling host. Both of those choices would have to wait though, because he first wanted to know more about what lay at the end of their road.

Three blood-red doors, side by side against the far wall of the dead end.

Like some of the previous doors they had passed, these

three bore brass nameplates, but unlike the others, these nameplates displayed a single letter, rather than a name. The door on the left was undersized, being only slightly taller than Naomi. Its plate bore a large letter **P**. The plate on the door in the center, which also happened to be undersized, displayed a large letter **F**. The door on the right was the most bizarre of any they had seen so far. It had been hung on its side, like a lying down rectangle rather than a standing one. It was also set several feet off the ground, keeping its nameplate at the same height as the previous two. This would prevent anyone from entering it without a bit of a climb if it was opened, which did not seem to be an option, because none of these doors had knobs. The plate on this last door was also turned on its side, but still easily legible. It was another large letter **P**.

Like the doors displaying quotations which they had passed through earlier, these had old-fashioned keyholes set in them, though these keyholes were larger and much higher up, being just beside the nameplates. There was a feint flickering glow coming through the keyholes, making it clear that something resided in the rooms beyond.

Graham had nearly forgotten the presence of the nearby child, when her words, obviously spoken more to herself than anyone else, reminded him of her presence. "Least ye be vexed…" she said, while staring off to her left. There, in the shadows, another misshapen melon could be seen, this one much furrier than the other, and now blessedly silent.

Those were the words written on the dog's collar, Graham recalled, and though it had taken him a few seconds longer than Naomi, he eventually attached the beginning of that old-fashioned saying to their current situation. The beginning of that saying was, "Peek not through a keyhole," though he was perplexed as to how someone Naomi's age would know such as saying.

Glancing at the third door, Graham mused that while he had no idea why anyone in their right mind would hang a door sideways, he did have an idea that the placement of the keyholes made one thing obvious. Whoever put these doors here wanted someone of Naomi's height to be able to see through those keyholes with as little effort as possible, if they wished. He turned to his smaller companion to find her staring at him, and the haunted look in her eyes told him she had come to the same conclusion. In yet another display of courage that Graham had come to admire her for, Naomi gave a sad smile, shrugged, made her way to the door on the left, and peeked through the keyhole.

He had been expecting her to take a quick look and then report back what she had seen, but she didn't. She stared for several minutes without speaking, fully engrossed in whatever mystery lay beyond, her tiny face illuminated by the peculiar glow from within. Her expression made it clear that she had completely forgotten that either of the nearby adults existed. He waited silently and patiently, though he felt his curiosity growing every second. Nearby, Celeste, who was working hard to appear uninterested, examined her fingernails from various angles with a sour face.

More unbearably long minutes passed with Naomi peering through the keyhole without moving or speaking. Suddenly, the child let out a gasp, bringing her hand up to cover her mouth in a display of alarm. Graham considered asking what it was she was seeing but decided it might be best to wait. He was jolted into changing his mind when she let out a shriek of shock and anguish which eclipsed everything he had heard from her today.

"Mom!" she wailed. "No!"

"What is it?" he insisted. "Is someone in there?"

She ignored him and continued to stare desperately through the keyhole for several minutes more, with her hands now pressed against the wood on either side of it, breathing rapidly. His impatience eventually exerted itself, and Graham reached out to her, intent on getting her attention whatever it took.

At that moment, Naomi turned away from the door with a disturbing blend of fear and confusion on her face. Her quivering lips were slightly parted, beads of sweat dotted her forehead, and her eyes darted back and forth rapidly, focusing briefly on and then away from the old man beside her. She seemed to be in the midst of what he had heard referred to clinically as *panic shock*. Having dealt with many others in a similar state in the past (though he oddly could not recall exactly who, when or where), Graham doubted she was actually seeing him or anything else her eyes appeared to rest on. She surprised him again by addressing him just long enough to hold up a single finger (wait!) before darting over to the middle door. Now looking as if she were sick, she put both hands over her heart and took a deep steadying breath and let it out before turning to peer into the second keyhole.

Graham waited as she had asked, though doing so was infuriatingly difficult. Thankfully, she spent much less time at the middle door than she had at the first, but when she turned away from it, she seemed even more confused and more upset than before.

"Naomi," Graham said in a hoarse whisper, struggling to maintain his composure. "What did you see?"

The girl only shook her head in answer without looking at him, apparently deep in contemplation, appearing far more like the child that she was than she had before. Her eyes drifted to the nameplates on the first two doors and then widened as if something unsettling had just occurred to her. She swayed slightly on the spot as both her hands rose to cover her mouth. "Oh my God," she said in a muffled gasp, before turning and darting to the last door. Once there, she peered through the last keyhole.

"Enough of this," Graham grumbled. He headed toward the leftmost door while speaking to Celeste over his shoulder. "I'm sure I don't need to tell you to stay put but stay put!" He didn't wait for a response, before turning to stare into the keyhole, through which he hoped to finally find the answers he sought.

The room beyond the door was completely dark now, with no sign of light or life. A frown creased Graham's brow, and he was about to make an angry inquiry to his smaller companion when a rectangular band of light began flickering on and off. It reminded him of the kind of illumination sent from vintage projection cameras like the one his parents once used to show old home movies. When blurry black images began moving across the rectangle of light, Graham realized he had been correct in his assumption. He was watching an old movie through a hole in a door. Without warning, the rectangle of light exploded forward, usurping all his vision and momentarily blinding him with its brightness. When his eyes recovered, he saw that he was no longer standing in the Southeastern Archives Repository dead end. He was somewhere else.

It was as if he had been dragged bodily into the shadowy realm inside the unseen camera. Everything around him was as black and white as an old Twilight Zone episode, yet just as lifelike and tangible as the world Graham had left behind. He even realized, once he got over the shock of being sucked into an alternate existence, that he was hearing sounds and smelling smells that did not at all coincide with the hallway he had just vacated.

I'm in the backseat of a moving car, Graham thought. *Or more likely an SUV, judging by the size.* He could smell coffee of the expensive variety, which he assumed probably meant some type of expresso or latte. He could also smell leather, again of the expensive variety, as well as what he was sure was one of those "new car smell" air fresheners. Amongst these odors, drifting past in random intervals, was the faintest trace of a vaguely familiar perfume.

The car's interior was warm, and he could tell that the heater was running dutifully to keep it that way, but he could also feel a slight chill radiating from the windows. The scene outside explained it. Brilliant white snow touched everything as far as the eye could see. It covered the ground, the grass, and the shrubs entirely, as well as most of the trees at least partially. It also lightly dusted the road as it drifted lazily down from the sky. He was admiring how believable this illusion was, when his attention was drawn by the sounds of two people in light conversation coming from the front seat. He did not recognize the voice of the woman who was driving, but he immediately recognized that of the girl sitting beside her.

"Where did your history teacher take your class again?" the driver asked. The question was followed by the sound of her sipping her coffee. Graham leaned forward to get a better look at the speaker and wasn't surprised to see a middle-aged version of the very girl with whom he had been traveling. The woman had one hand on the wheel and the other on a cup that bore a Starbucks label.

"The Archives building near the courthouse," answered the cheerful little voice Graham had come to know well. He turned and stared directly into the face of Naomi, who interestingly enough, was wearing the exact same Heaton Academy uniform she was wearing now, and she wasn't hued in black and white. She was, in fact, the only bit of color in this oddly colorless world, and her shock of brown, burgundy, and blue made it obvious who this movie was all about. "It was so cool," Naomi continued. "I met Mrs. Weldon there! You know, the old lady whose family owns the hospital? She's really nice, and I helped her find out some stuff about her family history from some records we found. She was so happy and so grateful. I think it would be fun to work there."

Neither of the front seat occupants seemed to be aware of Graham's presence, and when he reached forward to get their attention, his hand passed right through them. *Alright,* he thought, understanding. *I'm a passenger, not a participant.*

"Ugh," Naomi's mother moaned. "Those Archive people are nothing but glorified librarians, honey. I thought you were aiming for Holme University?"

"I am!" Naomi chirped. She turned in her seat, and for the briefest of moments, Graham thought she actually saw him, but he was mistaken. Her glance moved past him and on to the seat nearby where two familiar objects lay. The first was a perfectly shaped, bright orange globe of a pumpkin, with a gnarled and twisted green stem extending from its crown. The second was a Hello Kitty backpack.

"Well, I'm not paying Holme University tuition for you to become a librarian, missy," Mom said. "You can go to West-lake State for that."

"You're not throwing out your ceramic pumpkin, are you?" Naomi asked, her eyes briefly turning to her mother. "You love that thing."

"No way," her mother said, taking a sip of her coffee. "Margie at work claims she can fix the hole in the back. She even offered to clean off whatever that disgusting stuff is growing out of it, but I keep forgetting to give it to her. It's been back there over a month."

"Aren't you supposed to have both hands on the wheel?"

Naomi said with a grunt. She was attempting to contort her body enough to grab the backpack, but the distance and her seatbelt wouldn't allow it. "Ten o'clock and two o'clock. That's what Gran says anyway."

"Why yes I am, smarty," Mom replied, giving a little shake to the cup in her hand. "But then I couldn't drink my espresso, could I?"

Sighing loudly, Naomi unbuckled her seatbelt, turned around completely, and finally managed to get her hands on the object she desired. Instead of pulling it into the front seat with her, she unzipped it and began rummaging around inside.

"Well, it makes me nervous with all this ice on the road," Naomi chuckled, obviously aware she had just made herself far less safe.

"Well, *you're* making *me* nervous," Mom squawked. "Now turn around and put your seatbelt back on, child!"

Naomi was making Graham nervous as well, and he attempted to help her with her search, but his hands kept passing through the bag.

"One second," Naomi cooed. "I just wanna grab my book."

"That creepy one about murder cults you've been reading?" Mom asked, sounding disgusted. "Swirling Indecency, or something?"

"A Spiral of Depravity," Naomi corrected with a laugh. "And no. I'm grabbing my sketchbook. I jotted down some ideas about what to get my roommate Catherine, and I wanna know what you think."

"Well hurry up," Mom insisted, taking another sip of her expresso. "I still can't believe the poor girl has never had a birthday party before. You sure she didn't grow up in some weird cult or something?"

"Pretty sure," Naomi said in an oddly somber tone. She finally got her hands on the object of her desire, to

Graham's immense relief, and she placed it on the seat beside her.

Something in Naomi's demeanor as she reached for her seatbelt made it obvious that there was a lot more to the story concerning her roommate than she was saying. It was also obvious that she was unsure whether she should share what she knew with her mother. In the end, her uncertainty didn't matter.

What happened next made Graham's heart feel as if it skipped a full beat and then leapt into his throat. In his line of work, he had heard many truly disturbing screams, but he had never heard one that he would have defined as bloodcurdling. That truth changed when he heard the scream that came from Naomi's mother at that moment, which consisted of three words strung together as if they were one.

"OHMYGOD!"

The scream was her instant reaction to a car which had suddenly veered directly into her lane, making a forty mile an hour head-on collision inevitable. Without thinking, Graham made a desperate grab for Naomi. He knew the attempt was hopeless, but he had no desire to see her tiny head shatter as it collided with the windshield, or worse, to see her body burst through the glass and onto the icy road beyond. Her mother dropped the cup of espresso, released the steering wheel entirely, and made her own frantic attempt to grab her child. Both adults failed.

Mom was unsuccessful because time and forward momentum just would not allow for the possibility of her success. Graham was unsuccessful because he was, as he observed earlier, a passenger, not a participant.

He shut his eyes to avoid being witness to a tragedy, but then something odd happened. At the exact moment of impact, everything around him stopped moving. Graham opened his eyes as he felt himself being thrown forward. He assumed his body would be exempt from the laws of physics in this reality and was shocked to find it reacting to the momentum of the collision even though nothing else was. While the surrounding world remained frozen in time, he shot forward and passed through the windshield, which showed no evidence of his journey.

He floated briefly in the space between the drivers of the two vehicles and when he passed the midpoint, time seemed to reverse itself. Graham likened this experience to someone pressing the *rewind* button on an otherworldly remote control, affecting everything in this existence but him. The damage done to both vehicles was slowly undone, they both moved apart, and the looks on the faces of the passengers changed from horror to shock, then from shock to surprise, finally returning to complacency. Graham passed through the windshield of the second car, and by the time he found himself seated comfortably in the seat behind the driver of this new vehicle, the car he had just exited was nowhere in sight.

Like the SUV he recently vacated, the front seat of this car was also occupied by two females. The difference in this situation was their age. The SUV had housed a mother and daughter pair. These young ladies both appeared to be teenagers. *High School seniors,* Graham's addled mind thought, judging by the books, papers, and backpacks haphazardly strewn across the backseat beside him. *Damn sloppy ones too.* Further inspection of the papers (trusting that they lay behind their respective owners) told Graham that the driver's name was Elizabeth Prater, and her passenger was Patricia Kench. *Why are those names familiar,* he asked himself? Before he could come up with an answer, a squeal from the front seat grabbed his attention.

"That fat ugly bitch!" Patricia shouted. "She snitched because she's jealous that he never gave her a second look."

"Who would," Elizabeth replied in equal exasperation. "She's trash."

There was a brief silence, and then in a more morose tone Patricia said, "The police spoke to my parents this morning."

"Mine last night," Elizabeth responded.

"They're supposed to come back tonight," Patricia said. "They want me to give a statement or something."

Elizabeth nodded. "Same here."

Patricia turned to look briefly in her companion's direction. "You gonna tell them you screwed him?"

Elizabeth gave her friend a wary glance. "Are you?"

In spite of himself, Graham had become so engrossed in their conversation, he momentarily forgot about this pair's future encounter with Naomi and her mother, but now the white Mercedes Benz sport utility vehicle was near enough for him to make out Naomi's tiny figure completely turned around, and out of her seatbelt. The last thing Graham saw before all the world became chaos, was the girl named Patricia giving her friend a nonchalant shrug.

Without warning, the small car was slammed from behind by a tremendous force.

Both Graham and the girls screamed as they were thrown violently forward, and Elizabeth, who had only two years driving experience and virtually no experience driving in snow, lost control of her car. Again, Graham found himself witness to the heartbreaking accident he was sure would result in at least one death, and again time seemed to stop at the moment of the collision. This time he was snatched backward rather than forward, pulled through the backseat and out the trunk as the events rewound themselves. When his disorientation passed he found himself in the backseat of yet another car.

Like the first, this car was a large SUV with a middle-aged female driver, but unlike either of the other cars, this woman was alone. She was having an extremely heated and particularly animated argument with someone on the other end of the Nokia cellphone she held to her ear. Her rant was equal parts screams and sobs, coming in loud short bursts, while tears ran unchecked from her puffy eyes. Graham winced as an explosion of words echoed within the small confines of this new vehicle, assaulting his ears.

"But they're looking for you now Glen!" the woman shrieked.

There was a brief pause punctuated by the silence, and then…

"They think something happened at the house, Glen! They think I knew!"

Another pause, more tears, a few sniffs, and then…

"All those times you said you were working late grading papers! All the times those girls came by for tutoring! Were you lying to me?"

Yet another pause, after which the woman slammed her fist onto the steering wheel as she wailed…

"What the hell are you talking about? Who the hell cares how they dress!"

Graham gasped as the vehicle lurched to one side and was amazed to see that his alarm was not mirrored on the face of the driver. Her current emotional state didn't appear to allow for concern over slippery roads, or her own personal safety. The only remaining bit of rationality in her mind that might have helped her get things under control did finally manage to focus on the correct object, but in an incorrect way. Just a few yards ahead, puttering along at a fairly safe speed for existing conditions, was a small car carrying two teenaged girls. Clearly written on the rear windshield of the VW Beetle in loopy white letters was the message "Lizzy's Ride! CLASS OF 1999!" In the seconds before the two vehicles collided, Graham witnessed a truly disturbing thing. The look on the woman's face slowly transformed from a glimmer of recognition to a spark of understanding and finally, into a mask of rage. It was a transformation Graham found horribly familiar. In his mind, a hate-filled voice echoed, "They owe me a life and they're going to pay! All the filthy little bitches will pay!"

In her current state of mind, it was quite likely that Clarissa was unaware of her fixation. With her foot firmly and unconsciously planted on the accelerator, Clarissa's SUV plowed into Elizabeth's car. There was no screech of tires to give the girls in the VW warning. There was only a sickening crunch before the Beetle veered violently off to the left.

Graham felt a familiar tug as he was once again snatched away, and time once again reversed itself. His ghostly journey through the backseat and out the trunk of what he now realized was a black Chevy Suburban, left him standing in the middle of the snowy road. With his vision unobscured by car windows, and his concentration unbroken by ranting drivers, Graham could now see that he was on a rather precarious mountainside thoroughfare. To his right were snow frosted pines and thick white drifts which veiled the mountain as it rose toward an overcast sky. To his left was a sheer and surely deadly drop, guarded only by a thin waist high rail of aged wood and rusted metal.

From his new vantage point between the slope and the fall, Graham watched the whole tragic performance play itself out. The impact of the Chevy drove the VW into the path of the Mercedes. The Beetle and the Benz struck head-on, while the Suburban slid into a deep drift. A tiny rag doll of a figure burst through the windshield of the Mercedes. The figure hit the road with a stomach-turning smack and rolled to a stop at Graham's feet. Sick with pity, Graham forced himself to look down on the now ruined face of his young traveling companion. Her tiny eyes were wide with terror, but they saw nothing. The mouth below them was an open oval of surprise that emitted no sound. Both her eyes and her lips were stained with blood, which appeared ominously black in this monochromatic world, despite Naomi's color.

Graham heard a gasp a few feet away and turned toward it. There in the snow, daring to appear shocked, stood Clarissa.

"You didn't even slow down you God damned bitch!" Graham bellowed, though he knew she could not hear. "You never even slowed down!" Furious, he took a step toward her, unsure what he planned to do, when a barely audible scream pierced the darkness. Both he and Clarissa turned toward the source of the sound.

Two heaps of twisted metal and broken glass locked together by a snarl of rusted guardrail was all that remained of the Mercedes and the Beetle. This smoking mass hung precariously on the edge of the drop, threatening to topple at any moment. No sign of life was visible in the crumpled mass of debris that had once been the VW, but a blood-streaked travesty was struggling to wrench itself from what remained of the Benz.

Her nose was horribly mangled and twisted to one side of her face. Her left ear was partially severed and hung from her head by a small sliver of skin. There was also a pristine white stalk protruding from her right wrist which couldn't have been anything other than broken bone, making the once beautiful woman a grotesque caricature of her former self. Each of these physical injustices leaked a viscous black liquid that ran slowly down her wrist and neck, staining the expensive clothes beneath. The level of pain the woman was experiencing must have been beyond belief. Still, Naomi's mother had only one concern–the welfare of her child, whose name she was now screaming with all the life she had left within her.

Something caused the pitiable woman to cease her wailing and turn to stare at the only other living person in the vicinity. Seeing this, Clarissa took a guilty step backward, shaking her head in denial of the accusation she thought she saw on the other woman's face. Both women appeared to be preparing to speak, though what they might have said to one another no one would ever know, for at that moment there was a loud crack resembling the snapping of a thick tree branch. Naomi's mother reached out with her uninjured hand, and then with cryptic silence, the entire wreckage dropped out of sight–Benz, Beetle, guardrail and all.

As if on cue the surrounding world began to dim. Graham assumed this meant that this nightmare illusion was coming to an end. The last thing he saw before being sucked out of the colorless world, was Clarissa jumping back into her Suburban (which had negligible damage), backing out of the snowbank, and driving away. She hadn't given the dying child in the middle of the road a second glance.

Nursing a heavy heart, Graham found himself back in the dead-end hallway of the Southeastern Archives Repository. The first thing that caught his eye was Celeste. She was staring at him, and her sly grin had returned.

Graham was about to ask her what the hell she had to smile about, when he remembered that the girl he had just seen dying on a snowy road was nearby. He turned to find Naomi in the same spot, gazing intently into the small keyhole set in the sideways door. Part of him desperately wanted to ask her whether the images he had just witnessed were true, while another part insisted that was a stupid question, because they couldn't be. The child he was staring at now bore no indication that she had been the victim of a forty-mile-an-hour head-on collision, or that she had passed violently through a car windshield. There were no scars on her face, her clothes weren't torn or bloody, and she was still in possession of the bag and the book, both of which Graham was certain had gone down the mountainside in the wreckage.

He decided it was best to know what lay beyond the **F** door before asking any crazy questions, so he reluctantly made his way over to it. This time, having an idea of what to expect, he took a moment to brace himself before peering through the keyhole.

After a few seconds of disorientation, Graham found himself once again thrust into an oddly realistic virtual world, complete with all the familiar senses, yet void of color. This time he wasn't sitting in the back of a luxury SUV or a teenaged girl's gas guzzler. On this occasion, Graham found himself standing ankle deep in newly fallen snow and surrounded by tall thin leafless trees, each of which bore small black notches on their flaky gray-white trunks.

"Aspens," Graham muttered, as a questioning crease knitted his brow. He remembered the first time he had walked through this out-of-place grove, all the while thinking how much some of those odd notches looked like eyes. "I'm in Pale Wicker Wood, south of town. But why…"

He paused when a flash of color caught his attention. Lying on the ground nearby, facing the overcast sky and partially covered with snow, was a young girl. She was dressed in her now familiar burgundy and blue, which could barely be seen beneath her large red fur-trimmed parka and pink tasseled scarf. Her posture was hauntingly similar to what it had been moments after the horrific accident Graham had just witnessed, except for her eyes which were currently shut.

"Naomi…" Graham groaned, wondering what new tragedy had befallen the unfortunate child.

Her eyes snapped open, making him wonder whether she had heard him. He was only certain that she hadn't when she sat up and scrutinized her surroundings but gave no reaction to his presence. Just as before, he surmised that he was a passenger and not a participant. Graham examined her face. In her eyes he saw an immediate recognition of her surroundings. He also saw sorrow far deeper than what her youth and innocence should have allowed. Sighing heavily, she wiped away a few errant tears with the back of her tiny fist and slowly got to her feet. She took a moment to rid herself of a few stubborn bits of clinging snow, and to adjust her now iconic backpack before heading off into the forest alone. Graham desperately wished to follow her if only to ease his conscience about letting a child walk alone into the forest, but his feet wouldn't move. Feeling a heavy sense of remorse, he watched her disappear into the distance leaving only a slight depression where she had lain and a faint trail of tiny footprints, both of which were soon erased by the snow.

Graham glanced around the empty wilderness, wondering if there was something else he was meant to see, when without warning everything went dark. The blackness surrounding him was thick and oppressive, and Graham was thoroughly confused. The other illusion hadn't concluded this way, so was this the end of the movie, or was something wrong? A sliver of panic began to creep its way into his heart as he wondered if there was any chance he could be trapped in this bleak colorless world forever. Then the light returned. He found himself once again standing ankle deep in newly fallen snow, surrounded by tall thin leafless white trees with trunks etched by small black notches–notches that were increasingly growing to resemble eyes.

"Aspens," he said, frowning in confusion. "Pale Wicker Wood..."

He glanced down. There on the ground lay the same

burgundy sweater vest, navy-blue pleated skirt, fur-trimmed parka and pink tasseled scarf, wrapped around the same little brown girl that had recently departed. As he watched, dumbfounded, Naomi awoke, cried, stood, and walked away just as she had before. It wasn't until the darkness and the light returned, bringing yet another Naomi that he truly understood, and that new understanding broke his heart.

"She's going to wake up every morning here in the snow," he whispered to himself. "Wake, walk away, die, and then relive the whole sad sorry mess, over and over again." This realization must have been the key to his release, because he immediately found himself back in the hallway standing before the door with the **F** set into it.

After staring at the door for several silent seconds, he eventually spoke his thoughts aloud. "F, for Future," he mumbled. With a glance at the first door he added, "P, for Past." He then turned to the child who was still staring intently into the keyhole of the sideways door, but he kept his next thoughts to himself. *What then, is she seeing now*, he wondered? *What was in her present?* Could it be the three of them standing in this very hallway, discovering the horrible truth? *No*, he surmised, because she had been at this last keyhole much longer than it would have taken to see something as simple as that. Whatever it was, he knew it couldn't be pleasant, because even with her head turned, he could tell she was deeply troubled.

"Finding those answers you were looking for?" asked a snide voice from behind. "Or perhaps you're feeling a little vexed?"

"Shut up," Graham spat without turning.

"You *were* warned," Celeste reminded him casually. "Both of you were warned, but you just had to know, didn't you, sugar? You just had to solve the mystery."

"I said shut up!" he growled through gritted teeth.

"Did it ever occur to you that perhaps that little clown girl was trying to help?" Celeste offered. "That just maybe she was trying to spare you both from the pain of knowing?"

Graham stood speechless, unable to respond to the woman's questions, because such thoughts as those had never crossed his mind. *And why should they have*, he asked himself? *All the puzzle pieces I managed to assemble, both sides and middles, implied a picture which did not in any way include tiny saviors dressed as dead clowns.*

"You aren't a sheriff, Graham," Celeste said, sounding shockingly compassionate and oddly weary. "Emmett isn't your deputy, I'm not a manager, and this isn't an Archives Repository. Everything here, *including you*, is exactly what she needs it to be, to allow her to remain sane just one more day."

Graham rounded on the woman, scowling fiercely, while fighting back a level of anger which he knew would soon cause him to do something he would surely regret. That this woman would dare try to pollute his addled mind with lies in a sadistic attempt to justify her heinous behavior toward that poor innocent girl was truly disgusting! He raised a threatening finger, which he was relieved to see wasn't a fist, and was about to utter words which were probably more appropriately coupled with the fist than the finger, when a harsh shout from the child nearby drew his attention.

"Kill me, Graham!"

Naomi's words shocked the rage right out of him.

"*What?*" he replied, certain he hadn't heard her correctly.

"I want you to kill me," she repeated. "I can't go on living like this!"

"But you said dying would just reset everything," he challenged, feeling uneasy. "We both just saw that through this here keyhole." He hated those words as soon as they passed his lips. In his mind, it sounded like the kind of whining he despised hearing from other people.

"Not if it's you," Naomi assured him in a detached sort of way. Her face was still pressed to the keyhole.

"I don't know about that," he said, shaking his head. It wasn't that he had changed his mind about doing whatever was necessary to end this, he told himself. This horrible God damned day had just made him weary of dealing out any more death.

"It's the only way this will really end," she said.

"And just what do you expect me to do," he asked, throwing up his hands in frustration. "Shoot you?"

"You could use the pillow," she offered, without turning.

"The pillow?" he said in a tone of utter confusion. "What pillow?" He had scanned the area thoroughly before they began their keyhole gazing, but Naomi sounded so certain when she spoke, she caused him to do so again, fully expecting to see a pillow nearby.

There was no pillow, of course, but his search had apparently amused Celeste, if her chuckling was any indication.

"Oh, Graham," the woman said in a pitying tone that sounded more like herself. "You still don't understand, do you sugar? But you will."

Graham ignored her and continued to focus on the child.

Naomi had fallen into silence again, and he assumed that something important must have happened beyond the keyhole. Several seconds passed, each one so pregnant with anticipation it possessed a physical presence. Without warning, a heartbreaking sob escaped Naomi's lips.

"Please, Graham!"

"Naomi, I just don't think I can–"

The child's distressed wailing interrupted him.

"No!" she cried. "Don't leave! I can't do this anymore! You have to end it! I'm losing my mind!"

Thoroughly bewildered, and equally unsure how to respond, Graham just stood there, speechless. He watched as Naomi took a few faltering steps backward with her face in her hands. When her back touched the opposite wall, she slid to the floor in a crumpled heap, sobbing. Graham took a step forward with the intent of consoling her as best he could but stopped when a movement to his left caught his attention. He turned in that direction and received a nasty shock.

The sideways door was no longer sideways.

Somehow, in the seconds that his eyes had been on Naomi, it had soundlessly and impossibly righted itself. It now looked identical to its fellow doors, with one exception. The keyholes on the other doors were still set at the perfect height for Naomi. The keyhole in this newly changed door was now set at the perfect height for him.

Like its asking me to come and take a peek, Graham thought.

"Well now that's a pretty obvious invitation if I do say so myself," said an insolently knowing voice from behind. After a brief pause, the speaker added, "…sugar."

"For the last fucking time, Celeste, shut up!" Graham growled without turning. His instinct had been to face the object of his venom when he spoke, but he did not want to take his eyes off that door, because he was harboring a secret dread that if he turned away it would change again, and when he turned back, he might catch it pretending no longer. He might catch it being something far darker than a door. Something more hideous than a simple passage from one place to another. Something hungry. He did his best to shake off these dreadful thoughts and instead focused on assembling the pieces to his puzzle.

If his assumption about the nameplates was correct, Naomi's present lay beyond the newly changed door, and judging by her current state, it was much worse than the hopeless vision of her future, with its promise of endless repetition, or the horrid vision of her past, which included the grisly demise of her mother. Seeing her finally give in to her sorrow was particularly troubling, because she had proven herself to be one of the bravest and most resilient people he knew, young or old. What then had finally broken her, he wondered? Seeing herself in this very hallway staring through that tiny keyhole and accomplishing absolutely nothing forever and ever and ever might be enough to do it, he thought, but he could think of worse fates.

This might, for instance, be one of those situations he had heard referred to as otherworldly. He might peer through that keyhole and find that the facility he had fought so hard to gain entrance to turned out to be some-thing, rather than some-place. Such a dark revelation would definitely make him reconsider little Halley-clown's place in the broader scheme of things, though he doubted he could ever think of her...of it, as helpful. Either way, the final obstacle, the largest and quite likely the most important pieces of the puzzle, resided in that room.

Standing here ruminating over his next move reminded him of a saying he had read from one of his favorite authors, Stephen King. Though nowhere near an exact quote, he was pretty sure it went something like this: When there are no other choices to make, hesitation benefits no one.

Though he believed this wholeheartedly, it didn't make those few steps he had to take toward his goal any easier. He did gain some solace in knowing that if he fully understood the situation, perhaps he could bring some sense of peace to the poor child lying on the floor.

With that thought in mind, Graham stepped forward and gazed through the keyhole of the final door, and allowed himself to be drawn into the world beyond. He allowed himself to understand the truth.

11

Graham was surrounded by a dark nothingness and silence.

Now that several uneventful minutes had passed within this shadowed reality, there was no point in denying it. His seventy plus years of existence had supplied him with an objectionable collection of unwelcomed sensations. Of these, fear was the most common and considering how often in life he stood on the edge of peril, that was understandable. It was unacceptable in his humble opinion, and it was unwanted, but it was understandable. Now, as he floated in an inky sea of nonexistence, all his feelings, including fear, appeared to have fled.

Now there was only a dark nothingness, and silence.

From somewhere within the void, Graham heard the faint faraway beep of an unknown machine. After a few more seconds of silence, he again heard the beep. Along with it came the low and somewhat pleasant hum of another diligently working machine, whose sound grew. Once the humming sound was well established, it remained constant. So did the periodic beep.

Graham slowly opened his eyes and then blinked and squinted against the unfamiliar glare of the nearby lights. When his eyes grew accustomed to the brightness, he glanced around. He found that he was slumped rather uncomfortably in a large leather reclining chair. This chair was set beside a bed, that appeared to be the focal point of a tastefully though sparsely furnished room which was about the size of a modest home office. He smelled the hint of what he was certain was some type of professional grade cleaning chemical hanging in the air, along with a faint trace of rubbing alcohol, or Betadine. Was he sitting in a hospital room then?

He believed he was, which was a bit of a surprise. He was also surprised to find that everything in this room was as filled with color as he was, though he wasn't quite sure why that was a noteworthy point. His sense of touch was another interesting point whose oddity lacked context, as he noted that he could feel someone else's warm slender fingers grasping his own. Though the owner of the hand lay unresponsive in the nearby bed, Graham was sure he sensed a bit of desperation in their grasp. The hand was the hue of cream-ladened coffee, and it was attached to a young woman who appeared to be in her mid-twenties.

Graham sat silent, giving his bewildered mind a few minutes to catch up with what he was experiencing. He felt that there had to be a bit of dreaming involved in the explanation of what was going on, especially considering that he had just awakened, but he couldn't quite nail down which exact parts of his recent experiences had been real and which had been imaginary. Though it was an exceptionally unsettling notion for a down-to-earth type of man, which he had always considered himself to be, Graham believed he may have just shared unconscious headspace with another human being, and worse, that this was likely not the first time. Accepting this, however tentatively, helped his mental fog to lift on other points as well. He could now recall, for instance, that dozing off was not an uncommon occurrence when he spent any extended amount of time in this room.

Staying the entire night, however, was exceedingly rare. In fact, last night may have been the very first uninterrupted late-evening to early-morning rest he had ever experienced here, though he wasn't certain "rest" was the optimal word to use.

This had undoubtedly been the longest of the dreams he had ever dreamt in this room, and while the earlier ones had many subtle (and many not-so-subtle) differences from this last one, there were far more similarities. There were so many similarities, in fact, that one might accurately define these shared dreams as *reoccurring*.

But why would that be, he wondered? Was there a lesson he was meant to learn from these dreams? If so, how many times had he failed to learn that lesson, and more importantly, at whose expense had he not learned it?

Feeling a growing sense of guilt building in his gut, he turned to the lithe figure of the young woman on the bed. *Whose expense indeed*, he thought, as he gently separated his hand from hers. He might not have answers to the other questions, but that last seemed obvious.

He was still contemplating what, if anything, he was meant to learn so that he might bring these apparent nocturnal wanderings to an end, when the door to the room opened.

"Good morning," said an amiable and somewhat familiar voice.

Graham turned in the direction of the voice and saw a face he knew well. Standing just inside the doorway, wearing sky blue nursing scrubs and holding two cups of coffee, was a tall slender young black man with a pleasant smile that seemed to say, *I'm pretty sure everything is going to be ok.*

"When I came by earlier, you were still asleep, so I didn't bother you," the young man said, stepping into the room. Mistaking the frown of thoughtfulness he saw on Graham's face for one of confusion, he set one of the cups he was holding down on a nearby counter and held out a hand, saying, "Emmett."

"You haven't been with us long," Graham said, taking the offered hand and giving it a firm shake. "But I remember you." Glancing at the nametag pinned to the newcomer's breast, which read **E. Tillman,** he added, "Tillman? Like that poor young man from Mississippi?"

"Close," Emmett said with a somber nod. "His last name was Till, and I'm pretty sure he was from Chicago."

"That's right," Graham agreed, returning the nod. "The murder happened in Mississippi. A damn shame. They shoulda given those two inbred hillbillies the chair. I'm Jonah by the way, though nobody calls me that. Folks round here just call me Graham."

"Pleasure to meet you again, Graham," Emmett said, smiling warmly.

"Likewise," Graham said, returning the smile.

After a nod to the hospital nametag clipped to Graham's shirt, Emmett asked, "What does the F. stand for?"

"Janice's little joke," Graham said with a wan smile, plucking the laminated rectangle of paper from his chest. It read **J. F. Graham**.

"Janice the Receptionist?" Emmett asked.

Graham nodded. "She's one of the few that knows," he said, "and it don't matter how many times I tell her not to put that initial on there. She does it anyway." After a moment's hesitation during which he considered keeping the information to himself, Graham said, "It's Felix, but don't go spreading that around."

"Sure thing," Emmett agreed. "Though I have to say, that's not so bad as far as middle names go. Better than mine anyway."

"What's yours," Graham asked.

"Merlin," Emmett said with a chuckle.

"That is pretty bad," Graham agreed.

"Oh, it gets worse," Emmett said. "That makes my initials EMT!"

They both laughed quite a bit after that, and Graham found himself feeling much more relaxed than he had felt in a long time.

"So, I guess I was destined to work in a hospital," Emmett said, shaking his head.

"Guess so," Graham agreed. A question popped into his head. Any other time he might have considered asking such a question to be a rudeness, but he had already shared an embarrassing fact about himself, and Emmett had established himself as an easy-going sort of guy. Besides, he was curious. "You weren't named after that poor young man, were you?"

"I was, actually," Emmett said with a laugh. "Momma said she did it so I would always remember how far black people have come since then, and how far we still have to go. I personally think telling me about it would have been enough, but that's just me." There was a brief lull in the conversation, which Emmett broke by saying, "Almost forgot!" He held out the coffee he was holding. "Thought you might want this. I've seen you grab a cup or two from the breakroom. Heavy cream and sugar, right?"

"Much obliged," Graham said, accepting the cup. "Now what's this 'life-or-death emergency–'"

Graham stopped midsentence, physically shaken by what he had been saying.

"Sorry?" Emmett said as he turned to retrieve his own cup and take a sip.

"…nothing," Graham muttered, looking flustered. "I guess I'm not quite awake yet."

"It's really kind of you to help care for the young lady there," Emmett said, nodding toward the nearby patient. "She's a bit of a celebrity, since she's been here for so many years."

Graham turned. In the bed lay a young black woman with a familiar cascading bush of dark curly hair surrounding a placidly beautiful face. Clear plastic tubes extended from plugs in her nose and throat, and needles in her arms, making their way to nearby machines that either provided life-giving sustenance or removed life-threatening toxins. A bracelet of white tape encircled her right wrist. Printed on it in large capital letters just above a barcode was a name. It read: NAOMI DOVE. Something about seeing her name stirred his emotions, and he turned away before he lost what little control he had.

"I was on duty when they brought her in," Graham said, scarcely conscious of his words. "Not head of security yet though." With a forlorn glance in Naomi's direction, he added, "She was just a little thing back then, barely thirteen years old. They brought her mother and the other two girls from the accident here too, but they were D.O.A.."

"I heard about that," Emmett said. "Hit-and-run driver caused the head-on collision that knocked them over the mountainside, right?"

Graham nodded grimly. "Yeah."

"And Miss Dove here survived because she was ejected from the vehicle?"

"Yeah."

"Ironic."

Again Graham nodded as he sipped his coffee.

Emmett sipped his coffee as well, and then said, "A friend of mine who works for State Patrol told me they thought locating the wreckage of the two vehicles that went over the edge would be easy, but it wasn't…"

"…and the only reason they finally found it," Graham said, taking Emmett's pause as a queue to step in, "was because of the out-of-place ceramic pumpkin they spotted lying near the huge tree hiding the wreckage."

"Like it was marking the spot for them," Emmett said, sounding disquieted.

"Like it was marking the spot," Graham agreed, sounding equally disquieted.

There was a brief silence, and then…

"I don't usually pay any mind to gossip," Emmett said, looking apologetic. "But this is so crazy I just have to ask. There's a weird rumor going around about how Miss Naomi there was found…"

"You mean the one about the wolf," Graham said, his eyes on his cup.

"So, it's true?" Emmett asked, openly incredulous.

Graham shrugged noncommittally. "There are some who believe it enough to keep it going."

"Okay," Emmett accepted, "but I heard that the guy who found her, I think it was the local Florist, Mr. Finkel, said he probably would have hit her if not for this huge wolf, and that it had been standing over her like it was trying to keep her safe and warm. Supposedly he said it refused to move even when he damn near ran over the thing, and that it forced him to get out of his car and help her."

"Old Ezra also said that it was bigger than a grizzly bear, and that it spoke to him," Graham muttered.

"Yeah," Emmett chuckled. "I guess that's why most people didn't take his story seriously."

"That and the fact that there haven't been any wolves in Georgia," Graham pointed out, "of any size, talking or otherwise, since before the pioneering days." After glancing down at the slender brown hand of the young woman lying beside him, he added, "Though Harborage County is known for being a place where weird things happen."

Emmett nodded thoughtfully at that last statement, and then said, "You called him Ezra just now. Do you know him?"

"Not well," Graham admitted. After motioning to an empty vase on the nearby stand, he added, "He brings Naomi flowers on the anniversary of the day he rescued her, which means he should be coming today with it being the twelfth and all. We talk if I see him, but I can count the number of times we've spoken outside of this place on one hand."

Emmett nodded and sipped his coffee. "Was the hit-and-run driver ever caught?"

"By me, in this very room as a matter of fact," Graham replied, surprising himself with this point, while knowing it to be true. "She convinced a couple of the nursing staff, that would have been Hargrave and Jyles, to look the other way while she snuck in to try and clear her guilty conscience. Found her in here ranting about her husband committing suicide, her life being ruined, and how the accident wasn't her fault, which of course was a lie." Openly disgusted by the memory, he added, "Almost had to use my Taser just to get the cuffs on her."

"Hargrave and Jyles..." Emmett mused. "You don't mean Celeste Hargrave and Dorian Jyles, do you? The former director of nursing and the former head nurse?"

"The very same."

"So, that's why they were let go."

Graham nodded. "That's why."

"And the hit-and-run driver?"

"A lady by the name of Clarissa Jareth, formerly Clarissa Hargrave. She and Celeste are cousins."

"What ever became of her?" Emmett asked, taking another sip of his coffee. "Prison, I assume."

"Prison," Graham agreed, nodding. "But she escaped the same year I retired from this place and hasn't been seen or heard from since."

"How'd she manage that?" Emmett asked, looking surprised.

"Story has it that she got ahold of something sharp and attacked several other inmates. She nearly killed one woman and injured a few others before getting herself beaten and choked out, and then going into what they believed was cardiac arrest. Apparently, she had some sort of heart condition which they were not equipped to handle in the prison infirmary, and the ambulance bringing her here skidded on the ice and ran off the road, another bit of irony I suppose and in the confusion she disappeared."

"That's some story," Emmett remarked. "Any idea why she lashed out like that?"

"Revenge," Graham said flatly. "I was told she had a violent altercation with those self-same inmates on her first day inside. It put her in the infirmary for weeks. She later claimed she had been pregnant, and that the beating caused her to lose the baby, but there was no proof to back that up." After taking another sip of his coffee, he added, "If I hadn't had my own altercation with her, I wouldn't have believed her capable of such violence, thin stick of a woman that she was."

Graham sighed and set his cup next to the flower arrangement on the nearby stand. He then got to his feet and stretched. As he did so, an old and battered library book, years overdue, slid off his knee and hit the floor. He stood there for a long moment frowning down at it as if it was some new and interesting species of insect. Seeing it immediately reminded him of the many other books, magazines, and newspaper clippings that were now sitting on the nearby coffee table, along with a partially completed jigsaw puzzle.

His memories slowly returning, he recalled that their main purpose was to help pass the long hours he spent at Naomi's bedside over the many years. He often read the books aloud, hoping they might garner a reaction from her, particularly regarding the book which had just slid from his knee, even though he considered its subject matter to be distasteful.

As he glanced at the table, he noted the tattered and yellowed edge of an old newspaper article peeking out from under the haphazard pile, divulging the sordid tale of the abduction and murder of ten-year-old Hailey Finch at the hands of the local serial idiot, Jasper Lee Dalton. Unlike the Daltons, who resided in the trailer park the next street over, The Finches had been kind, caring neighbors, who could always be counted on for a friendly wave and a pleasant smile. Graham could recall at least one occasion when he had confronted Jasper about his casual drives through the area, which in hindsight coincided with the time when Hailey and her schoolmates headed home. It was heartwarming how that albino Pitbull puppy of hers would trot out to the bus stop to meet Hailey and walk her home, and Graham remembered hoping it would grow to be enormous and become a menacing deterrent for anyone with questionable motives. But unfortunately, it never got the chance to grow, and neither did Hailey. Jasper had seen to that, on an afternoon when Graham had been elsewhere, and no matter how many times he told himself there was no way he could have known such a thing was going to happen, he continued to blame himself for not doing something to prevent it. Putting down rabid animals like Dalton hadn't been his job. His job was hospital security, not general law enforcement, though sometimes he wondered whether he had missed his true calling. As difficult as it still was to admit it to himself, Hailey's fate had been someone else's failure. Regardless, he continued to feel guilty. He was wondering exactly when and why he would have read such a thing out loud in this room when he was drawn out of his navel gazing, as his late mother would have put it, by the sound of Emmett's voice.

"Do you always read the same things to her?" Emmett asked.

Graham nodded and bent to retrieve the book with an audible grunt. "Pretty much," he said, sitting the book beside his cup of coffee. With a gesture toward the currently silent TV which hung on the far wall, he added, "Unless we're watching the news, that is." The words on the cover of the book, clearly visible in the light of the desk lamp, read: *A Spiral of Depravity*. "She had it with her on the day of the accident," he said somewhat defensively, seeing Emmett eyeing the ominous title. "It was her grand-aunt Candace's idea. She thought that hearing me reading it might help Naomi find her way back."

"Yeah," Emmett said thoughtfully. "I heard that your voice is the only thing that's ever gotten a reaction from her."

"Don't know if I'd call it a reaction, exactly," Graham said. "I just stuck my head in to give Candace my condolences, and when I spoke, Naomi twitched in my direction. Not sure why. I'd only ever met the child once or twice before, because her mother, Kenisha Dove, and I often ate lunch in the same restaurant, and she would sometimes bring Naomi with her. That twitch was probably just a coincidence, but Candace never thought so."

"You seem to have known the family pretty well," Emmett remarked.

Graham nodded. "I grew up with the two sisters, Candace and Ellanor. Kenisha liked to pick my brain about the old days during lunch, when she found out I knew her mother. A beautiful, beautiful woman, Ellanor was, inside and out. I guess you might say we were kinda sweet on each other when we were young, but I didn't have the balls to do anything about it. Back then, what they used to call miscegenation…" Here Graham paused and gave Emmett an inquiring look, silently asking if he was familiar with the word, while also making it clear that he didn't wish to be more specific. Emmett gave a brief nod, so Graham continued. "…was very taboo in these parts. Still, we were friends, but not a day goes by that I don't regret my cowardice. Anyway, last thing Candace said to me before she passed was, 'Promise me you'll take care of my grandniece, Felix.' I did, so here I am."

"Every day?" Emmett asked, seemingly impressed.

Graham nodded. "I don't work here anymore, so…" he ended the sentence with a shrug.

"But you're still on the hospital board though," Emmett pointed out. "So technically, you're one of the bosses."

"I am on the board," Graham grudgingly admitted. "But I think it's a bit of a stretch calling me one of the bosses. Got no idea why Mrs. Weldon-Hyde appointed me, or why she insists that I remain on it, other than her saying she needed someone 'down to earth' in the position."

"She must trust your judegement," Emmett offered, sipping his coffee.

"She must," Graham conceded. "You mind handing me one of those fresh pillows from the closet?"

"Not at all." Emmett set his coffee aside long enough to do as he was bid, adding, "I'm pretty sure it was changed a little while ago, though."

"It was," Graham agreed. "But I always change it for a new one when I leave just the same. Makes me feel like I've actually accomplished something." He slowly and gently placed the new pillow under Naomi's head with loving kindness, setting the old one aside.

"Well, I need to run," Emmett said, turning to the door. "See you tomorrow?"

"Sure thing," Graham said. "And hey, thanks again for the coffee."

"Don't mention it," Emmett said. "Thanks for the conversation."

They both gave the customary parting nod, and Emmett exited. The door silently slid shut behind him, leaving the old man and the young woman alone. As Graham stood there looking down at Naomi's seemingly lifeless body, many repressed emotions fought their way to the surface of his consciousness. In his mind, Graham replayed the last things Candace Brown had said to him ten years ago in this very room, from her wheelchair, before complications from diabetes carried her to her reward.

"Way back when we were all a whole lot less ancient," Candace began, "Right around the time Ella was set to graduate from Spellman, 1966 this would have been, she returned here to spend a few days with you while you were fixing up your grandmother's old house, didn't she?"

Candace's tone, which he always thought of as motherly, even back when they were children, was now also accusatory. Graham recalled nodding his answer, feeling more than uncomfortable discussing such things with her, much less doing so at the bedside of Ellanor's comatose granddaughter. He and Candace had never gotten along well, and he was pretty sure he could count the number of conversations they had in the past on one hand, good or bad.

"Ella probably didn't tell you this," Candace continued, "but a year earlier, she met someone down in Atlanta. He was a successful Morehouse graduate student from a wealthy black family, and he wasted no time expressing his intentions to her. She liked him quite a bit, and she knew he was exactly the kind of man my parents had prayed she would find when she left Harborage, but my sister spurned his advances because there was someone else she preferred. So, she came all the way back to Harborage, alone, without letting even her family know she was coming, because she needed to know if that person felt the same way."

Having no idea what the point of this conversation was, he remained silent and listened, though a frown of irritation etched its way onto his brow.

"While El was back in Harborage, your momma paid you a surprise visit," Candace continued, "which shouldn't have been much of a surprise, considering that you had been shunning that Dorothy Miller woman she had set you up with."

Dorothy Miller, he mused ruefully. Now there was a name he could have done without hearing. That had been a bullet dodged if ever there was one.

"Apparently, Dorothy had been expecting a marriage proposal from you any day," Candace said, regaining his attention, "and she was quite put out to find you entertaining some colored girl in your home…overnight. So, she ran to your Klan-connected momma and spilled all the beans."

Here Candace paused, obviously allowing him the opportunity to refute anything she had said. He didn't, because he couldn't without lying, so he remained silent. Eventually, she continued.

"I'm sure it ain't necessary for me to remind you of all the colorful words your momma used when she came in and saw my sister wearing one of her own momma's old dresses and eating breakfast off her good china," Candace said in a casual tone, "or what happened when your momma tried to rip that dress off my sister. Nor do I need to remind you that you completely failed to defend my sister against your momma that day."

"The biggest regret of my life," Graham admitted, gravely.

"Is it really, Jonah?" Candace asked, using his given name for what may have been the first time ever, instead of her usual name for him, which had simply been, "white boy." And was that a hint of sorrow he heard in her voice? If so, it came as a surprise. Sorrow from someone who would have preferred that he had never laid eyes on, much less spoken to, her sister? He had his doubts. Before he had a chance to answer, she said, "If that's true, I'm sorry, but I'm about to give you a much, much bigger regret." After pausing in preamble to what was certain to be bad news, she said, "You likely have no idea what your momma did after she ran my sister off that morning, but let me fill you in. You see, Ella was devastated by your failure to stand with her against your momma," she said. Though Graham genuinely felt he deserved this woman's scorn, he found himself wishing she would stop saying he had failed, however true it may have been. "In fact," she continued, "to say she was devastated is understating it. She was also too ashamed of what had happened to seek solace at our parents' home, where she might be forced to answer embarrassing questions. Some-how, your momma seemed to know exactly where Ella would go. My guess is that you had something to do with this." After seeing his face redden in apparent shame, she nodded and then added, "So, not long after my distraught sister arrived unannounced, your momma also showed up at my door."

Graham, who had no idea this had happened, was genuinely shocked by this, and looked it.

"I didn't think you knew," Candace said sourly, "though I have wondered what you thought had happened, considering how angry your momma must have been when she left you. Allow me to tell you how that morning went for my sister and I." Candace paused a moment, readjusted herself in her wheelchair, and then took a deep breath before returning her eyes to his. "After demanding to be let in lest she burn the God damned house to the ground, your momma informed us that she had been kind enough to leave her shotgun in the car. She also said that the only reason she hadn't used that shotgun during the earlier confrontation was because she didn't want nigger blood all over her mother's wallpaper. Apparently, your grandmother really adored that wallpaper. Your momma then told us that since Ella couldn't seem to get it through her thick God damned head that she was ruining your life, she was gonna have to ruin a few lives herself. She said that she was going to head home and make a few phone calls. The first would be to the foreman of the factory where my husband and I had worked for years. According to your momma, nigger workers were a dime a dozen, so they could stand to lose a few. Her second call would be to your daddy, whose job would be to light a few fires, being sure they were near my momma's home, and a few of her neighbor's homes as well. Her third call would be to a 'truly deranged individual,' her words not mine, that she called Opossum, whom she would demand repay a debt to her by bringing her three fingers from the first nigger child he could quietly get his hands on." At this point, Candace's tone changed slightly, and she sounded almost introspective. "That last bit truly terrified me," she said. "Considering your momma's own less than pleasant temperament, I couldn't imagine what kind of person might fit her definition of 'truly deranged.'"

Here Graham could remember shuddering at the memory of the revolting individual his parents called Opossum, who made Jasper Dalton look like a schoolyard bully.

"All that other stuff had been said to us both," Candace continued, "but then your momma turned and spoke directly to El. She said she would make sure that all the victims of these crimes would be told why those things happened, so they would know exactly who to blame. 'I don't give two shits in a bucket whether anyone goes to jail over it either,' your momma said, 'though I know none of them boys will anyway. What you need to know is this: All those folk gonna be just as out of work, and all those other folk gonna be just as homeless, and which ever nigger kid old Opossum puts his hands on gonna be just as fingerless or whatever the hell else Opossum decides to do to 'em, cause it ain't no telling with Opossum...unless you get the fuck out of town, and stay gone! Leave Harborage and leave my baby alone!"

After a long and reflective silence, Graham said, "That's why I never heard from her again."

"That's why you never heard from her again," Candace agreed, adding, "thank God. And I'll own up to part I played, drilling into Ella's thick skull how damned lucky she was for being given the chance to keep the shit from hitting the fan, because I never doubted for a second that your momma meant every single word she said."

Graham didn't doubt it either but made no comment.

"That's your grandbaby over there, Jonah," Candace said unceremoniously, nodding to Naomi.

"*What*," Graham nearly shouted, unable to hide his shock.

"It's what tends to happen, when two people spend a few secret nights alone," Candace said in what Graham was finding to be an increasingly annoying casual tone. "That wasn't just any old stranger you used to have lunch conversations with over cheese-grits and sausage. That was your daughter, and I know that you know when her birthday was, because her coworkers threw many a shindig for her in that same crappy little diner, with you in attendance. Had you bothered to do the math, you might have figured it out yourself. I suppose you should consider those lunches to be a bit of God's mercy, otherwise you might not have ever known your own daughter, considering what just happened."

"But why didn't El–"

Dwarfing his own, Candace's rage could not be contained.

"Don't you dare ask why my sister didn't tell you!" she shouted, jabbing her finger up at him menacingly. "Don't you dare! Not after what your crazy ass momma and the rest of your psychotic kin put us through! You think her threats were all we ever had to put up with? You think the beatings and the lynchings were just unfortunate misunderstandings, or that the burning crosses were just neighborly yard decorations? You have no idea about the dance and shuffle we're forced to do to try to hold on to what little we own without looking more successful than our white neighbors, lest we provoke another Tulsa or Rosewood or Oscarville!"

Graham knew that any comment from him, even one of agreement, would only make her angrier, so he held his tongue, particularly after hearing the name of that last town, whose dreadful fate he had heard joked about by his father and others. Yet he seethed inside, conflicted over whether what Ellanor had done had been justified.

"You had the opportunity to show my sister what kind of man you were willing to be," Candace hissed. "She had no reason to think that would change if you knew you were a father."

After taking a moment to calm herself, Candace returned

to her casual tone. "Ella married that man I mentioned. Ellington Harmon was his name, and he was a good man, who cared for Kenisha as if she was his own. He had two other children from a previous relationship, but he and Ella never managed to have any together. Those others were, and still are, two of the laziest, most spoiled rotten little shits I've ever met in my life, likely due to their gold-digging mother being jealous of Ella. They were a disappointment to their father in almost every way, so Kenisha, who never asked for anything, ended up being his favorite. When he passed, he left everything to Ella, because he knew she would take care of everyone else, as she did. His oldest children would have just pissed their inheritance away. Ella did consider getting in touch with you when Ellington passed, particularly after hearing that your momma was no longer around."

Following a meaningful pause, she added, "My condolences." Graham chose to nod rather than respond verbally.

Candace took a deep breath, sighed, and then said, "The cancer took Ella quickly, and even on her deathbed she couldn't bring herself to tell Kenisha the truth about you, not that she was in any condition to do so. After she passed, it became my responsibility." Her scowl softened considerably, and the look Candace gave him held more than a hint of sadness. "I never intended for your daughter to die without knowing who her father was, but I'm not going to apologize for it either. I know you think I hate you, but that isn't so. I don't like you, but I don't hate anybody, including your crazy racist momma, God rest her misguided soul."

Though Graham's jaw clinched as he struggled through a conflicting mix of emotions, he remained silent. Candace also seemed to be struggling with a near overwhelming wave of feelings, which she was making no attempt to hide.

"I don't have long for this Earth, Jonah," she said, as tears made their way down her brown cheeks. Despite her struggle, her voice remained as unwavering and strong as ever, and without being told, Graham knew she wasn't crying for herself. "I'm not gonna let them cut anything else off of me, diabetes be damned," she said, nodding to the vacant space where her foot once was. "I plan to exit this God forsaken world eatin' and drinkin' whatever makes me happy, so it's gonna be up to you."

She turned to the bed where Naomi lay, and said, "That baby there deserves to know her granddaddy, but she won't have the chance if certain family members get their way. When Ella died, she left all her money to me, against everyone's wishes, and there was a hell of a lot to leave. That was years ago, and they're still fighting me for it. I loved my sister, I loved my niece, and I love my grandniece, so I'm going to do what I know Ella would have wanted. I'm gonna leave as much of it as I possibly can…to you."

She raised a hand as a wordless request for him to set aside the protest she saw on his face, eventually adding, "If I don't give it to you, none of it will go toward keeping that baby there, under the best care money can buy, because the gold-digging filth on every side of the family will stick her in the cheapest piece of shit hospice they can find, so they can split the money amongst themselves, and let my grandniece rot. So, you swear to me, Jonah Felix Graham. If you ever loved Ella, you swear to me right now that you'll find the courage to fight both my family, and my in-laws, and keep my grandniece, *your grandchild*, right here where she needs to be, because I wouldn't put it past any of them to try and have her taken off the machines keeping her alive. Swear that you will come here every single day, and you'll talk to her, and read to her, and hold her hand. Swear that you will always do whatever needs to be done, because I don't even want to think about her suffering under someone else's care."

So, he had sworn, and he had found the courage to fight.

This ended up being no small feat, because the amount of money concerned turned out to be in the millions. At a time when violent murders occurred over far less money on a near daily basis, allowing one broken little girl to quietly fade away didn't even register as an ethical dilemma for the other people involved. Naomi's fragile existence meant nothing to them, but it meant everything to Graham.

Using any of his newly acquired wealth on himself gave him an unbearable sense of guilt, so he continued to spend much of his days working for the hospital as head of security in order to pay the bills, until he retired and joined the Board. He devoted most of the remainder of his time to caring for his grandchild and thoroughly resented any time he was forced to spend fighting to hold on to the money.

"Don't be tempted to offer the slightest bit of it to any of those people to get them off your back," Candace had warned. "I'll hand out as much as I feel any of them deserve. No amount you give would be enough to satisfy them anyway, and you'd quickly find that there is no end to the line of mouths begging to be fed." She also advised against making the contents of his Will, which he had a lawyer sit down with him to create the day the money was transferred to him, known to anyone in either his family or hers, lest he find himself the victim of an untimely accident. Through it all, he kept Naomi in the best long-term care that Weldon Memorial had to offer, and he kept his promise.

After ten years of visits had come and gone (or 3,653 days if certain dying ravens were to be believed), with Naomi continuing to cling to life somehow, he began to question his own mortality, amongst other things. He resumed his seat at his grandchild's side and took her hand. His mind felt clear for the first time since waking up this morning, and new questions began popping into it. How was he able to share dream-space with her by holding her hand when he fell asleep in this room? That was the first question, and he real-ized he had asked himself this many times before. The second was, why was he always robbed of his memories once he entered that dream-space?

He was prevented from asking the one person who might have an answer to this mystery anything about the first ques-tion due to the facts surrounding the second, though he supposed the major brain trauma she had experienced in the accident played a part. Injuries aside, something truly extraordinary, something genuinely magical, was occurring here. The first night he had been drawn into her dream, it had frightened him badly. So badly, he had to force himself to return to her room, and several weeks went by before he allowed himself to fall asleep in her presence again.

He had never shared his experiences with anyone else, because he feared he would return to her room to find that she had been spirited away to some secret government lab to be studied, poked and prodded for the remainder of her days.

Once he had become accustomed to what he eventually began to think of as his nocturnal jaunts with his grand-daughter, he noted a disturbing trend. The dream Naomi was privy to bits of real-life information she had no business knowing. Worse, her subconscious appeared to be using these bits of knowledge to shape her imaginary world. Without meaning to, she was integrating the fears, hopes and regrets of anyone she had encountered, or any conversation she happened to overhear.

This unfortunately included all the traumatic emergency room experiences of the many doctors, nurses, and orderlies in the facility, as well as the sorrows of her grieving friends and family members which had visited. Thus, it was not a wonder to him that her dream world was so dark and filled with terrors. Her broken mind was struggling to make sense of the disjointed facts it was receiving as best it could, and in its desperation, it shoehorned someone who (familial roles aside) was technically a stranger, into the role of small-town sheriff when he occasionally popped into her manufactured existence, because that's what she needed him to be.

I wouldn't care about the how's and the why's of it all, if you were having pleasant dreams, he thought to himself. *But you aren't.* Unbidden, he found himself wondering for the first time since this all began exactly what Candace had meant by him doing "whatever needs to be done," and about Naomi "suffering under someone else's care." He hadn't given those words a second thought back then, but he did now, and he felt that there may have been something more unsettling hidden in those words. As he contemplated this, he recalled the last things he heard the child say just before he exited her dream prison.

Kill me, Graham.

"You don't really want that," he said aloud, knowing that somehow that frightened little girl peering through that small keyhole could hear him.

I want you to kill me. I can't go on living like this.

"Euthanasia is a crime," he pointed out, feeling his emotions rise. "There would be an investigation."

Not if it's you.

That was probably true, he thought. There had, in fact, been several attempts by various family members to have Naomi removed from life support, arguing that such an existence was selfish and cruel on his part, and that she would not have wanted to live in this vegetative state. That they actually wanted to prevent her constant care from eating away at what they saw as their inheritance was no secret, because Graham, being true to his word, had always been there to point it out as often and as loudly as necessary. They brought their lawyers, of course, but his were better. Now, after years of heated arguments, at least one of which had turned physical, he knew he would be the last person anyone would ever accuse of ending Naomi's life.

It's the only way this will really end.

"How would I even do something like that?" he asked.

You could use the pillow.

And now her earlier words finally made sense. There the pillow was, in his hands (he must have grabbed it unconsciously), waiting to be used. The mere thought of doing such a thing disgusted him, but he found himself equally bothered by the thought of leaving her this way. In the end, he couldn't bring himself to do it.

"No," he said through quivering lips.

Please, Graham.

Knowing he had to leave before he changed his mind, he tucked the pillow under his arm and turned to go. "I'm sorry," he whispered, and with a bit of dread, knowing what the circumstances of such a visit would entail, he sadly added, "See you tomorrow."

As he exited the room, he told himself that the sobbing voice, begging him not to leave, pleading for him to end this, and insisting that she was losing her mind, was a figment of his imagination brought on by a guilty conscience. By the time he reached the elevators at the end of the hall, his vision blurred, and his wizened cheeks dampened by tears, he almost believed it.

———

Sometime later, a young girl awoke in a snow-covered glade. The trees surrounding this glade were Aspens, seeded here centuries ago by early pioneers who during their explorations much farther north and west had been enamored by the pristine white of the bark. Having not only survived but thrived against all odds in the southern heat, the contrast of these saplings against the larger, darker pines prompted later colonists to christen the area, Pale Wicker Wood.

The girl on the ground struck even more of a contrast against the unblemished snow than the Aspens did against the pines. She wore a burgundy sweater vest and a navy-blue pleated skirt that could barely be seen beneath her large red fur-trimmed parka and pink tasseled scarf. Though her eyes were shut, tears slowly ran from the corners. When she sat up and opened them, they reflected an immediate recognition of her surroundings as well as a deep sorrow. Sighing heavily, she wiped away the tears with the back of her fist and got to her feet. She took a moment to rid herself of a few stubborn bits of clinging snow and adjust her backpack (which bore the animated likeness of a certain familiar feline), before heading off into the forest alone. A moment later she was gone, leaving only a slight depression where she had lain and a faint trail of tiny footprints, both of which were soon erased by the newly fallen snow.

One, again.

Graham was troubled.

Now that he correctly identified the feeling, there was no point in denying it. He had always done his level best to avoid what his mother had referred to as wool-gathering, feeling it was a general waste of time, but today he couldn't stop himself. Some irresistible urge demanded a bit of introspection this cold winter morning, so he reluctantly gave in.

Forty years as a law enforcer had supplied him with an unpleasant bounty of unwelcomed emotions. Of these, fear was the most common and considering how often his chosen line of work required that he place himself in danger, that was understandable. It was useless in his humble opinion, and it was unwanted, but it was also understandable. Now, as he sat peering through the windshield at the morning sun glinting off the newly fallen snow clinging to the hood of his patrol car, he recognized a fairly new emotion invading his typical countenance of pessimistic disinterest. Now, he was troubled.

"Something's wrong in this town…"

E P I L O G U E

Ezra Finkle pulled his Fiat onto the now paved shoulder of the road on almost the exact spot where he had skidded into a snowbank ten years ago. The weather was nearly as chilly as he remembered it being back then, but unlike then, there was no snow today, likely due to the issue he heard some of his customers discussing, which they referred to as global warming. Differing weather aside, from his car window Ezra saw one unmistakable similarity between that day long ago and today. The similarity was something he had been both hoping for and dreading, and he prayed that his rapidly beating heart would not choose this moment to abandon its duty after over eighty years of satisfactory work.

The paved shoulder area had been created to offer visitors a place to safely park their vehicles opposite the slightly more picturesque side of the road. A waist high guard rail was installed along the side with the stunning view of the mountain slope, to help those visitors feel safe. None of this was designed with sightseeing in mind, though quite a few people did take advantage of the opportunity the clearing provided to pull out their cameras with the intention of using them. Most people changed their minds when they realized the area was a memorial to honor the three people who had lost their lives on that very spot. Three roadside plaques were on prominent display here, reminding visitors of the unfortunate accident that occurred mere moments before Ezra had arrived that day. While the plaques were the old man's destination, they were not his only goal, at least not this time, and he had to take a moment to mentally prepare himself before he could exit his car. As he stepped out and winced when the seasonal chill made its presence known, he felt it was quite fitting that such an event should occur, with this being the tenth anniversary.

Ezra's rapidly beating pulse and shortness of breath caused him to stop a few steps away from the memorial, and it took him several minutes of prayer and concentration to calm himself before he could continue. He eventually got moving again, telling himself he would see this through even if it killed him, literally. Though it took much longer than it ever had before, he did manage to reach the memorial, and on doing so he thanked God for giving him strength.

Having visited these plaques on several previous occasions, Ezra did not need to read them to know what was written on each, yet he always did, as a show of respect. Before doing so, he tugged the glove from his left hand using his teeth and secured it in one of the many pockets of his goose down parka. He then pulled three charmingly smooth river stones from another pocket and placed them in his right hand. Looking slightly embarrassed, as if his actions were being judged (which he was certain they were), he cleared his throat and read aloud.

"In loving memory of Patricia Kench, beloved daughter." After saying this, he placed one of the stones on Patricia's plaque using his bare left hand. Next, he said, "In loving memory of Elizabeth Prater, beloved daughter," and repeated the ritual. Last, but certainly not least in his mind, he said, "In loving memory of Kenisha Dove, beloved mother and daughter," and he placed the final stone on her plaque. He then lowered his head and said, "May all their memories ever be a blessing."

Though the plaques were set in alphabetical order from left to right based on the victim's last name, Ezra had chosen a different order of recognition. His order was youngest to oldest based on birthdates, because while none of these lives lost was any less a tragedy, he had always believed that a tragedy was worsened when it involved a person whose life barely had the chance to begin. Also, he wanted Naomi's mother's plaque to be the last he touched before leaving, because he felt he had a more personal connection with her, even though he had never met her.

With that task complete, Ezra glanced down at the land surrounding the memorial and sighed. He knew that before his next visit, should he be fortunate enough to live that long, his lovely, hand-picked stones would join their equally beautiful predecessors on the ground amongst the common rocks, but this was not the only thing that bothered him. It was seeing the remains of the numerous flowers which had been left at the base of each plaque that had added to his melancholy. Most of them were quite old and desiccated, though some appeared to have been placed there earlier today.

"It is not our way to leave flowers at memorials or graves," Ezra said, returning the glove to his hand, which was beginning to grow numb with the cold. "But I always feel a little guilty not doing so, considering what I do for a living." With a laugh, he added, "If I were a gambling man, I would be willing to bet that most of these came from my own shop."

With the slightest hesitation, Ezra turned and lifted his

head and looked into a now familiar pair of moon-yellow eyes. He hadn't seen those eyes in 10 years, but he had never forgotten them, and he hoped that what he was observing in them now was warm recognition. He allowed the moment of soundless salutation to pass before he shifted his gaze to take in the entirety of the enormous beast. He had been an old man when the two were first introduced, and was an even older man now, with numerous aches, pains, and wrinkles to prove it. The she-wolf, however, did not seem to have changed in any way. He still found her just as imposing and just as frightening, but he also found her just as beautiful in a mystifying sort of way. Ezra longed to hear her speak.

That he wished to hear his dear mother's voice again was not the only reason for this, though he did wish that quite badly. He also desired some sense other than his sight to prove he wasn't imagining her, because he had endured quite a bit of ridicule over the years, from the many people who knew his story and declared him to be a dotty old codger, however heroic they might have also believed him to be. Tortured by the conflicting emotions, part of him desperately wanted someone else, anyone else, to see the wolf, while at the same time he also desired to keep this astonishing creature, who in his mind proved that real magic existed beyond childhood, all to himself, because it made him feel special in ways he couldn't explain. That aside, the cold was blunting his sense of smell, which wasn't as strong as it once had been and therefore useless in this instance, and he dared not touch the beast without her permission, so, taste aside, hearing was the only sense that remained.

He had dreamt of several such meetings with the creature over the years, where they spoke of many things, though never shoes, or ships, or candle wax, cabbages or kings. Such nocturnal encounters always left him feeling saddened and more alone than he had been before going to bed, making him certain that if he had ever managed to find the beast again, it would surely be an agreeable encounter, not unlike reuniting with an old friend. Now, he was beginning to think he had been mistaken.

"The child still lives," he said, hoping to touch on a subject which might interest the she-wolf. "Though, sadly, she remains asleep and is no longer a child. Thankfully, she has a devoted caregiver, who, interestingly enough, happens to be her grandfather."

He believed he saw the beast offer an almost imperceptible nod but nothing more.

"I visit her in the hospital from time to time," he said, turning to the memorial. "Seeing her lying in that bed, so quiet and so still, has caused me to contemplate things I have never considered before. I think about her quality of life, such as it is, and what kinds of thoughts may be going on in her mind. I pray they are only ever pleasant thoughts, but I do fear otherwise. I also wonder whether keeping people in her situation alive is for their benefit, or our own, and whether it is ultimately a mercy or a cruelty."

Ezra turned back to the beast, and was almost certain he noticed a reaction, though it was even more subtle than the nod. Reflected in its huge eyes was a hint of the sorrow he had seen just before it departed after their initial meeting. It was a heartbreaking sorrow. One which he had come to understand quite well during his lifetime, yet he also thought he saw something else in those eyes.

"Forgive me if I am being presumptuous," Ezra began but then paused, feeling unsure of himself. A frown creased his brow as he considered the beast. After clearing his throat, he continued though tentatively. "Perhaps I am mistaken, but would I be wrong in believing that your presence here that day was no mere coincidence?"

The beast lowered its head, and if he had seen such a

gesture performed by a person, Ezra would have easily defined it as guilt. He was certain that the beast had not caused the accident, because the woman who had been responsible had confessed, though only after she had been caught. Regardless, he was just as certain that this enormous oddity of nature somehow blamed herself for what had happened. *But why would she*, he wondered?

He was on the verge of asking this, when the she-wolf's ears pricked up unexpectedly, and the beast turned its huge shaggy head in the direction of the road. When Ezra followed its gaze, he saw nothing out of the ordinary on the nearby road. A familiar voice accompanied by a woeful echo brought his attention back to the beast. The voice was in no way pleasant, and in many ways unsettling, but it brought a smile to Ezra's wizened face and tears to his eyes.

We unintentionally opened a door into her mind when we chased away death that day.

As the beast spoke, something impossible occurred. Right before his eyes, the creature began to shiver, and her appearance blurred. In a matter of seconds, she went from being an enormous wolf to a typical-sized wolf, and then to something else entirely. The most frightening part of the transformation was when she pushed herself up to stand on her hind legs, briefly giving Ezra the impression that he was standing next to a werewolf pup. By the end of the wondrous change, her snout had diminished considerably and her fur had vanished entirely. Her newly acquired skin was much paler than his own, making her many freckles quite visible. She had wispy auburn hair which hung to her shoulders and appeared to be about the same age Naomi was when the accident occurred. She was also clad, head to toe, in the burgundy and blue uniform of Heaton Academy.

"I have weakened myself in my many attempts," the girl said, in the exact high sweet voice one would expect to hear from a troubled teenaged girl. "But I cannot close that door. I fear that all manner of unwanted things may have slipped inside and are affecting her rest." With a look of sorrow that mirrored the one Ezra had seen on the wolf, she added, "This means I bear responsibility for any and all suffering she endures."

"Please..." the old man said in a near whisper of utter astonishment, which set his heart galloping once again. "What *are* you?"

"In the courtyard of my school there is a tree," the once-wolf now-girl said, ignoring the old man's question. "They call her The Violet Lady. You know this tree?"

"I...I do indeed," Ezra stammered. "My dear wife, Yissika, may her memory ever be a blessing, graduated from Heaton."

The girl turned her attention to the road as if she expected to see something there. This echoed what she had done as a wolf earlier, though now she added a frown and a squint of her eyes that made it clear she was calculating a problem in her mind. Ezra turned to follow her gaze again, and again found the road empty. When he turned back, he was shocked to find himself once more standing in the shadow of the enormous wolf.

*Look for us...*The wolf began in its customary growl, but then corrected itself. *Look for* me *there, if you wish to learn more. If you wish to understand, and perhaps to help.*

To his surprise, the she-wolf smiled. Such an expression was wildly out of place on that lupine face, but he appreciated it just the same. Before he could think of how to respond, the once-girl again-wolf turned and moved several paces away. It lowered itself into a crouch, waited a moment, and then sprung over the side of the cliff with the grace of a cat, disappearing just after a car turned the corner. Ezra winced as the driver came to a screeching halt while swerving into the parking space dangerously close to his

Fiat. A young lady, perhaps in her early twenties, whose appearance placed her country of ancestry as one of the eastern Asian nations jumped out of the car.

"Mr. Finkle!" the young lady shouted, pointing toward the cliff and sounding out of breath. "Mr. Finkle, oh my God, did you see that? A huge animal just jumped over the edge!"

Feeling an immensely comforting sense of exoneration, Ezra smiled as he considered what the most appropriate day would be to visit a student at Heaton Academy.

The End.

The Never Trilogy continues with Book II: Whether or Never

ACKNOWLEDGMENTS

Special thanks to the following family members, friends, and colleagues, without whom this would not have been possible: Sheika Kendi, Dr. Tanya Nayo Clark, Dr. Roslyn Nicole Smith, Yolanda Webb, Suzi Kaplan, Barry Kaplan, Marnie Marra, Venessa Giunta, John Hartness, Melissa McArthur, Stuart Jaffe, Darin Kennedy, Theresa Glover, Maggie Schill, Scott Hawkins, Lucy Blue, Erin Penn, and of course my mother, Faye Clark.

ABOUT THE AUTHOR

Ojé Kendi is a Metro Atlanta based writer of supernatural horror and suspense, an artist of all things strange and disturbing, and a wanderer of shadowy forest paths. He began his story-telling journey long ago, while guiding his friends and family through fantasy worlds as a Dungeon Master, creating realms that were probably a bit darker than they were intended to be. The comment he recalls receiving most often on his grade school report cards was, "wastes too much time daydreaming,"–a fact which he didn't regret then, and doesn't now. He spends most of his evenings with his lovely wife and 3 cats, most of his nights with his laptop and his stories, and most of his days dreaming, still. *The Twelfth of Never* is his debut novel.

FRIENDS OF FALSTAFF

Thank You to All our Falstaff Books Patrons, who get extra digital content each month! To be featured here and see what other great rewards we offer, go to www.patreon.com/falstaffbooks.

PATRONS

Dino Hicks
John Hooks
John Kilgallon
Larissa Lichty
Travis & Casey Schilling
Staci-Leigh Santore
Sheryl R. Hayes
Scott Norris
Samuel Montgomery-Blinn
Junkle
Vickie DeSantos
Quincy J. Allen
Allison Charlesworth

Thank You for Supporting Independent Publishing!

We believe that you should be able
to read your books, your way.
That's why this Falstaff Books
print edition includes a digital copy
at no additional cost!

Just scan the QR code with your device,
follow the directions on Prolific Works,
and enjoy!
You can also join our newsletter when prompted,
and never miss an awesome Falstaff Release!